The Ka of Stephen Charles

Tom East

Benybont Books

https://www.benybont.org/
First published 2023
Copyright © Tom East, 2023
All rights reserved.

ISBN 9781916297395

To Edmund, Ping, Annabella, Joseph, and Claire

I acknowledge with gratitude the comments and suggestions on the text during its writing from Edmund Humphreys, Joseph Humphreys, Sam Kates, and Jack West.

CONTENTS

Prologue

Think of me as 'Steve Charles' or 'Martyn Bedford', if you must have a name. Neither are what we've ever been called, nor are they anything like the names we were given when we were born. Not one of the names used here is real. Each one of them, even the lesser ones like 'Will French', formerly a Prison Officer in HMP Wandsworth, is an invention.

You'll see later, if you read on, why I – let's just talk about Martyn Bedford for the moment – have no intention of using the right names. The locations are also something I've also played fast and loose with. Oh, most of the places are real enough but… Well, it'll be no good looking for a dismal childhood home anywhere near Alnwick, if you get my drift.

What about the things you're going to hear about? Did they happen, or did I make those up, too? It'd be no good my telling you they're the unvarnished truth from the horse's mouth – or perhaps I should say *horses' mouths*. You probably wouldn't believe a word. Well, that's your business.

You'll have to decide for yourself.

[1] Stephen

'Your luck's really in tonight, Stevie, my boy.'

This was Al, who was scowling at me from the opposite side of the chipped table in Bernie's back room. Any one of us could see that he wanted my inconvenient luck to go away. And I at least was sure Al wished I'd go away, too,

'It's about time I won something,' I said.

It was unusual for me to stand my corner in this way, but it was indeed high time for fortune to smile upon me for once.

I'd been a member of Bernie's card school for nearly six years. In fact, I'd joined within months of starting work in the wallpaper factory straight from school at the age of fifteen. I regularly lost half my wages every Wednesday night, thanks to Bernie. He was the one who'd outraged Al by inviting me to play cards with them.

Occasionally, the older ones would let me win a few Bob, just to try to keep me interested. Even then, I'd never won much more than a quid in a single evening through all the time I'd played.

'Right. I'll pay to see your cards,' said Den. 'Your good fortune can't hold forever.'

Den was the only one I could think of as a friend. It was he who found me the job in the factory in the first place. Working there meant long tube journeys every day from my room in North Ruislip to the factory in Parva-vale and back, but I could find nothing better.

There wasn't much work in a place like North Ruislip for boys of my kind. Anyone with sense would have moved to Parva-vale, but I never claimed to have much sense. I wanted to remain in North Ruislip, where I was born. Goodness knows why I should have felt that way about the place. North Ruislip had done nothing for me.

If I was honest, I'd have to say I was disappointed when I heard Den say he wanted to pay to see my cards. Ideally, I'd have liked the three of them – Tony had already turned his rubbishy hand in and looked more than ready to make tracks at any moment – to gamble away a bit more of their pay into the pot that would soon be coming my way.

Still, going by the look on his face, it was clear that Den had just tossed in his last half-crown. Anyway, the hour was getting late. I'd have to make tracks myself soon if I was to have any chance of catching the last train home.

Nine Card Brag was our regular game. This was the dicey one where, at least by the rules we used, you had to win all three tricks to claim the hand and with it the pot. Ours had been building up throughout the evening.

Luck was needed, yes, but so was skill in making up the best three-card tricks you could manage in a short time. Above all, you needed to know exactly when to hold your nerve and when to chuck the cards in. A lot of people had won or lost a lot of money through failure of nerve or sheer bluff. Sometimes it was simply a case of them trying to ride their luck too hard.

Tonight, it looked as if Lady Luck was going to be on my side big time for the first time in my life. I was the only one of the five of us to have won two tricks in a hand in this evening's long game. What's more, I'd done it no fewer than seven times. Now it seemed certain that at last I was going to go one better and win three tricks, and so the whole game. Then all that money on the table would be mine.

My first trick of the hand was on the table before me. It had been a prial of three nines. Nothing could beat that. The second, now lying face-up alongside the nines, had been, incredibly, another prial, this time of sixes. The pot had been growing like a living thing before us for at least the past hour and a half.

Everyone there, including Bernie, normally the coolest customer I'd ever met, was getting edgy. Unusually, no one had managed to win all three tricks in a hand since the beginning of the evening. By this time, more cash had been built up than I'd seen in any one place in the six years since I left school.

What none of the other four yet knew was that I still held the ace, the two and the three of spades in my hand. A fabulous running ace flush. Such a thing was unheard of. I was sure to win. My glance switched between the cards I was holding and all that money on the table. It was all I could do to stop my hand shaking. It was unbelievable. I savoured the moment.

'Come on Steve,' said Den. 'I've just paid to see you, mate.'

'One, two, three, on the bounce,' I said, laying my cards down on the table. As I expected, no one could come anywhere near this. The closest was Den, who reluctantly laid down his ordinary – it seemed ordinary on that night – Jack Flush. I'll always remember Den's three cards and my fantastic running flush. Al and Bernie could offer nothing better than pairs of some description. This was more the sort of thing you'd expect for a third trick.

Talk about poker faces: only Bernie, who regularly played in other, bigger schools, and was a professional compared with the rest of us, tried to maintain anything like an impassive expression. A dark shadow crossed Al's face and he flashed a look of what I could only think of as pure hatred in my direction. Young Tony looked aghast. He'd joined the school only two weeks before and I guessed he wouldn't be here next week. Poor Den, the only one I thought was worth his salt, paled when he saw the cards I'd put down on the table.

A muscle twitched right in the middle of Al's right cheek as he watched me sweeping up all that money from the table between my trembling fingers. Bernie had added thirty shillings, in the form of a quid and a ten bob note just a few rounds ago. He'd taken nearly all the silver. Most of the pot was now in pound notes. There were at least twenty of them, plus four glorious fivers.

Al would have physically prevented me from gathering up the money if he dared, but these were my winnings, won fair and square.

Even he wouldn't have tried to snatch the cash with everyone else watching.

'You little turd. You should be in the army. They'd make a man of you if anyone could do such a thing. Fighting for my country, I was, when I was your age.'

This was Al's constant gripe, this army and war business. He never seemed able to remember that most of the men of his generation had also been in uniform, not so many years before.

Even those of around my age, most of whom were doing, or had already done, their National Service in peace time, he disparagingly referred to as 'toy soldiers'. People like me who had, so far at least, been lucky enough to avoid the call-up altogether, he held in utter contempt. He never hesitated to show his feelings. Not Al.

'You know the medical board turned me down for National Service a couple of years ago,' I said. 'This wasn't my fault. It's just the way things happened.'

'How much did you give them for a favour like that? No wonder you never have any money, shorty. Anyway, they'll be catching up with you soon, don't worry. I've heard they're going to reclassify every last man jack of shirkers like you. They'll enjoy having a pretty little boy in the barrack room. Give the boys something to do on long nights like the ones we're having now.'

Al laughed at his own jest.

The worst thing was, both things he said might be true. It all depended on the person you asked. Some thought the government was going to do away with National Service altogether – this was what I heard Harold Macmillan promising on the wireless a month ago. This might have been nothing more than electioneering from the old guy – you can never trust these politicians. Others said the high-ups were going to make it tougher on people like me who'd been lucky enough to miss out first time around.

And we'd all heard the horror stories about those barrack-room nights.

Tony Seebles caught my eye. He looked miserable. The poor devil would be eighteen next week. He didn't know when he might receive an enlistment notice, travel warrant, and postal order from the Ministry. These didn't now arrive with the clockwork regularity they once did, but the poor boy's call-up papers might be lying there on his doormat any day now. If Tony was one of the unlucky ones, a few weeks after the postman's knock, he'd find himself one Saturday in a Ministry of Labour place.

I remembered only too well when this happened to me, not so long ago. It was only the medical that had saved me. Before the lad knew where he was, he might find himself being whisked away for basic training in some dismal camp like Aldershot.

We'd both heard all the stories about what the army had the nerve to call basic training.

'That's enough,' said Den. 'We've been through all this a dozen times. Things are different these days from the way they were during the war, thank goodness.'

I was grateful to Den for saying this. He'd fought in France himself and I knew he'd had no picnic. Someone had told me he'd been wounded at Dunkirk, although it wasn't a wound that was visible to anyone in any way.

Those times were something he never talked about. I knew he'd refuse point blank to speak about any of this if I asked him directly, so I never did. Funny thing, although Al was always mouthing off about the war and soldiering, he never spoke about his personal experiences, either.

'Right,' said Al. 'Whatever you say, Dennis, me old china. Next hand, then. It's your deal, mate'.

'I'm skint.' Den looked guilty at his response. 'I haven't got a halfpenny to last me the rest of the week. No dinner for me tomorrow. Count me out.'

'This is all too big for me,' said Tony. 'You all told me a tanner was the maximum stake.'

So it was, normally. But on this night, we'd all got carried away. It was Den I was most worried about now. He'd lost more money than anyone and looked as if he was ready to walk out of the front door and straight under a bus, if only he could find one still running at this time of night.

'Here, Den,' I said, pulling out a pound note from my left-hand pocket. This was where I kept my 'normal' money. I suppose it was superstitious of me to want to keep this stashed separately from the card money I would neatly fold in my wallet and put tidily in my right-hand pocket in a moment or two.

It did make it easier to count my winnings – more usually my losings – in this way. I suppose this might have been one reason why I did it, although in truth it was nothing more than a superstitious habit.

'You're not going to take charity from a little squirt like that, are you, Den mate?' said Al.

Den's worried expression changed into a frown, but he didn't respond in any other way, apart from nodding briefly to me when he took the money I offered.

Bernie shook his head to show he was out, too.

'Well, I never thought I'd see the day. Looks like it'll be just you and me for a final hand, then, sunshine.' Al leered at me, menacingly.

'I've got to go,' I said. 'My last train leaves in twenty-five minutes. I always get going at about this time. You all know that.'

'You've got to give a man a chance to win his money back, shorty. Bernie will let you sleep on his floor, won't you Bernie? You can walk to work from his place in the morning. Get yourself a decent breakfast in the works canteen for a change. Bernie, you can play along with us, or you can sit and watch for a laugh. Whichever you like.'

Bernie looked at me, spreading his hands in apology. As if I wanted to play another round of cards with Al!

'Sorry, chum. I need to be out at least an hour before work in the morning.' Bernie tapped one side of his nose. 'Got some private business, to look after, see?'

'Looks like you'll be sleeping in the station tonight, titch.' Al laughed. 'Unless you'd like to find a swanky hotel for yourself, that is. You might win some more money yet. No stake limit at all from now on, right?'

'You get yourself on that train, Steve,' said Den. 'We'll clear up for Bernie. We can all walk home easily enough.'

Al shot a hostile glance in Den's direction when he said this. I didn't need any further invitation. I rose on wobbly legs – I was really frightened by this time – and stumbled over to Bernie's front door, pulling on my jacket as I went. I stuffed the money into my pocket. I could put all those notes and coins away properly in my wallet once I was on the train. If only I could make it safely as far as the station, that was.

*

Outside, there was a heavy mist. It couldn't yet be called a fog, although there was surely one heading our way. There wasn't a soul in sight. My footfalls on the pavement made far too much noise for me as I half-ran down Lyndhurst Road. Several times, it seemed I could hear the alarming sound of another, heavier, tread behind me. Each time I thought I'd heard something, I stopped and looked over my shoulder. Each time, I saw nothing and heard nothing more than the echoes of my imagination. Eventually, the steps seemed to fade away from my hearing or imagination, and I pressed on towards the station. It felt a long way ahead.

Could I count on Den restraining Al from coming after me? Dennis Smith was no slouch, but Al was hot tempered, and a known bruiser into the bargain. As I'd slipped out of Bernie's front door, voices were already being raised. I had recognised Bernie's high-pitched voice joining in with the others.

Would he take Al's side against me – he'd lost a lot of money himself, too – or would he stick up for me, as I hoped Den would? You never knew where you were with a man like Bernard Albeck.

Young Tony must have been wondering what he'd let himself in for. A tanner maximum stake! My stake now felt much higher than this. Alarming images of me, a beaten-up mess, spending the night under a hedge with empty pockets – or worse – were haunting my every moment.

My greatest fear was that Al, as a local, would know some shortcut to the station from Lyndhurst Road. Den would hardly be likely to have any reason to try to stop Al if he walked out of the front door calmly, saying he was off home, too, even if Al stood up only a minute or two after I'd gone out into the misty night.

Al might have raced ahead by some unknown route to overtake me. If he'd done this, I'd encounter him in some quiet byway on the only way I properly knew that would take me to the station.

It was all I could do to stop myself breaking into a full run. But, if Al had decided to lie in wait for me in some secluded spot, I didn't want to let him know of my approach, so I tried to content myself with a brisk walk.

About a hundred yards from the station, I decided to cross the road and from the other side divert from my usual path and go through the park – this was more of a small green with benches around its edge, but I was fairly sure I should be able to pick up my road from near the back gate.

The park itself might make an ideal hiding place for Al, but he'd be unlikely to have gone so far out of his way. There might be an advantage for me, though. Taking this slightly longer route would mean I'd be approaching the station from the opposite direction, one that Al probably wouldn't expect. I was pleased with my plan and began to draw breath more easily as I started to make my way towards the park's front gate.

Then, just as I reached the edge of the park, I thought I heard the footsteps again. Hoping it was nothing but my nervous imagination once more, I paused by the edge of the park and listened.

The footsteps kept coming, more clearly now. Not that they could ever have been far behind me, even though I couldn't properly hear as well as see anything through the thickening mist.

Without thinking about what I should do for a moment longer, I dashed into the park, flinging myself down behind a bench and a drooping shrub.

This wasn't anything of an adequate hiding place, but the mist was now thickening into a fog, and all I could do was hope for the best. There was nothing else for it but to keep as still as I could. With a bit of luck, Al or whoever it was, wouldn't glance too far to his left as he passed.

The footsteps drew closer. Their pace was leisurely. This wasn't what I expected. I thought Al would quicken his step, or even break into a run at this point. I was terrified, to be honest. My heart seemed to beat in time with the unknown rhythms on the pavement. These drew level with my hiding place. Then the sound passed.

I raised my head slightly. It wasn't Al walking past, although it was someone else I recognised. Jim Corcoran was ambling along the road. Like me, he lived in North Ruislip. He hadn't lived there for long, and wasn't someone I could say I knew, even though he lived in lodgings only a few streets from my own.

Nor was he anyone I wanted to know. His tall figure, shifty eyes, and something about his whole bearing, made me suspicious of him. Mind you, on this night I'd have been suspicious if the Angel Gabriel had walked past me.

When I was satisfied that Corcoran's back had disappeared into the mist, I stood erect again, uncomfortably aware of the damp patches on my knees and elbows. Then I decided to wait for as long as I dared before going on, directly now, in the direction of the underground station.

*

With alarm, I suddenly realised I'd misjudged things badly. In the mist, I'd underestimated the walking distance from the park to the station. The squeal of the train's wheels on the metal of the rails was sounding long before I'd come even close to the station entrance.

I had to sprint the last twenty yards. Even then, I only made it because the platform I wanted was the one nearest to the station foyer. I barely managed to squeeze through the train's sliding doors as they closed.

My plan had been to get on a different car from Jim Corcoran, but there he was, sitting there large as life. He barely looked up at my face as I made my clownish entrance. Perhaps he hadn't seen my ridiculous performance properly. With a bit of luck, he might not even have recognised me in Parva-vale. After all, simply because I happened to know him by sight and name, it didn't follow that the reverse was true.

*

Even though I could hardly change tube cars at this stage, I made sure I took a seat as far from Corcoran as I could, near the other end of the compartment.

This wasn't only because I was so nervous about everything. I wanted to sort out my money – up until that night, the most I'd seen, let alone possessed, in all my young life – without doing it under the gaze of anyone.

I waited until we'd passed Greenford and Northolt stations before I even began the task. When I did, it was the first thing I'd enjoyed doing since raking in my winnings from Bernie's table.

It didn't take me long to tidy up the money, even though I tried to make the job last as long as I could. Soon I had the pound notes and fivers folded neatly in the wallet and the silver in my right-hand jacket pocket. My 'normal' cash, minus the pound I'd given to Den, was in my left-hand pocket. I was really loaded. It was the first time ever I'd had any real money.

The train rumbled into the outer edges of North Ruislip. Even in those days, it was a well-off area, although you wouldn't think so going by the dark shapes of the buildings and the mainly unlit streetlamps at the side of the line.

Anyway, I was anything but a typical resident of the suburb. The part I lived in wasn't the poorest, but I had only one small room I could call my own. For this privilege, I paid a rent I couldn't afford. I really don't know why I was so keen to live here once I was old enough to get out of that children's home, other than that I was aware North Ruislip had been the place of my birth years before.

This knowledge was the only real bit of a 'normal' family life I possessed. I have no idea who my father was, not even his name. One day, not long before she decided to swan off with an American airman in 1942 or 1943, my mother, whom otherwise I remember only as a warm but erratic shadow, came over all weepie and told me that, before the war, she was going to marry my father. Even then, she still wouldn't tell me what his name was.

The only other thing I remember her saying to me was that, before the wedding could take place, he went off to join the army, muttering something about 'making the country safe for my family first of all'. Sounds romantic, doesn't it? Well, it wasn't bloody romantic for my mother and me.

Things in Europe were already starting to look bad when he joined up in 1938, I've since read, but he became a member of the forces long before there was any real need for him to wear a uniform.

Then, soon after the fighting really got going, he went and got himself killed at Dunkirk. He died a hero, is what I think my mother said to me. Whether any of this is true or whether it was another case of my unstable mother romanticising, I wasn't sure. A fat lot of good had it ever done for me, either way.

*

As the tube was drawing up to the platform North Ruislip tube station, just as I was about to rise to my feet, I had an unwelcome surprise.

'G'night, mate,' said Jim Corcoran, nodding with what seemed like a smirk to me as he passed me on his way towards the tube exit door to my right. He'd walked the extra distance down the compartment just so he could say that. *Bastard*, I thought.

He wasn't my mate. In fact, these were the first words he'd ever spoken to me. Once or twice in the past, I'd thought about nodding hello to him on the street, but the look of him had always put me off. I wasn't going to start talking to him as if he was someone I wanted to know now.

Then, quite suddenly, as the train was braking, he turned around and walked back towards me.

'Oh,' he said. 'I've been meaning to give you this for weeks. It's important. Read it later and we'll have a chat about it when you're ready.' He placed a creased brown envelope in my hand.

I looked up at the greasy curls smearing his dirty collar. He'd sported his hair long well before this became the fashion. His eyes were shifty and his skin sallow. How could I even begin to want to know him?

All the same, I was nervous about the way he was looking so intently to see what I was going to do with the envelope. I tried to smile as I pushed it into the inside pocket of my jacket. Only then did he turn around and head for the exit doors of the train, now screeching to a halt at the platform.

Getting off the train at the last moment I could, just as the doors were about to close, I waited a full five minutes more to watch him cross the footbridge and so be out of my sight, and out of my mind. He was probably returning from some shady deal in Parva-vale in connection with the dodgy second-hand car business I'd heard he operated.

I pulled from my pocket the envelope I'd just been handed and tore it open. It contained only a small piece of paper with tiny, neat handwriting. I read: '*We need to talk. I have something important to tell you. Come to me at number 12, Cypress Close on any weekday evening as soon as you can. Jim Corcoran.*' That was all it said. Well, I didn't want to go anywhere near Cypress Close. Confused, I thrust envelope and note back in my pocket.

When I was happy the coast was clear, I started to clatter up the metal steps of the footbridge. At that moment, heavy raindrops started to fall through the haze. I had no overcoat so knew I was going to get drenched as I walked home. As always, every step I took across the span of the metal bridge made a loud clanging sound.

The cold mist, even though I couldn't say it was as nasty as the smogs I remembered from my childhood, was thickening despite the rain. It felt as though it was seeping directly into my bones as I walked. I pulled my jacket collar up in a fruitless attempt to get some protection from the elements.

I'd been thinking of Al's jibe about National Service since I'd arrived back in North Ruislip. Not for the first time, I wondered if my life was all worth the trouble.

North Ruislip station is close to the end of the Central Line. It still is part of the tube or underground system. I don't know why they insist on calling the thing by those names. Most of the London Transport system runs above the ground for miles before it reaches this far west. People grumble about the state of things now. Back in 1959 they were abysmal. We were only fourteen years away from the war, don't forget.

The ill-lit cars weren't at all like today's sleek if overcrowded carriages. They contrived to be both low slung and old fashioned. They would rock unhappily in their slow progress over the rails. You'd find nothing like a lift or escalator in stations like North Ruislip.

If you wanted to cross over to the other side of the tracks, as I always had to do when I came home from work or caught the last train home from Parva-vale after cards on a Wednesday, the only way to do it was by slogging over the metal footbridge.

At that time, and for years past, the card school I belonged to had met once a week, every week without fail. I should have become used to these dispiriting ends to my Wednesdays. I never did get used to them. Even this night, when in my pockets was more money than I'd ever seen before, didn't feel so vastly different from all the others.

The world was supposed to have been going forward in the later nineteen-fifties after the bleak years of post-war austerity but, if it was, the better times were passing me by. Wednesdays were my only regular nights out. I had no girlfriend, no family, and no close male friends. My tedious job in the wallpaper factory in Parva-vale wore me down. It paid peanuts and treated its shop floor workers like monkeys.

This was the fag end of the last Wednesday in the month: 25th November 1959, to be exact. I remember the date so clearly for three reasons. The first was that it was just two days after my twenty-first birthday. These were supposed to be special days marking your coming of age back then. Someone was supposed to give you the key to the door. In fact no one, not even Den, had so much as mentioned my special day in work. I'd spent the entire evening alone in my lodgings.

The second reason was that – I could still hardly believe it – I'd just come from my big win at cards in Parva-vale. The total of forty-four pounds, two shillings and nine pence may not sound like anything these days, but it was over six weeks' wages for me at the factory at the time. For a moment, I allowed myself to hope this money would somehow be enough to change my dreary life.

The third and most important reason I remember the date was that this was the moment when my life did indeed change, although not in any way I'd fondly imagined. I had no clue of what was to come as I was crossing the metal span of the footbridge.

In the wallet inside my pocket, I knew there were four fivers, twenty-two oncers, and five ten-bob notes. There was also some loose change. I recall fingering the embossing on the half-crown, as well as trying to count the twelve sides of the Joey when it happened. The thought of all that cash was starting to cheer me up a bit, although nowhere near as much as I expected it to. I was rubbing the Joey really hard. That I remember clearly.

It sounds really stupid, but I was thinking about that little coin – it was only worth threepence, or not much more than a penny in decimal currency – as if it were some sort of magic lamp from the Arabian Nights stories. Anyway, it was surely concentrating on this that caused me to miss my footing as I stepped onto the downward flight of steps.

It all happened so quickly. One moment I was playing with the coins in my pocket, the next I was flying through the air. For a split second I was, believe it or not, surprised rather than frightened. Then, my spine and the back of my head rattled excruciatingly painfully against what seemed to be each one of the metal steps.

After a momentary bright light as I landed on my head at the foot of the staircase, my world suddenly went black. It was all over.

Except that it wasn't all over. It was only just beginning, you might say. Starting with a series of blurred and confused images, I found myself looking down from mid-air upon my prone body at the foot of the bridge. I seemed to be looking downwards from a high place. My neck was awkwardly twisted around, enabling me to plainly see blood oozing from a deep gash on my temple. I must have cracked my skull against the metallic steps in the fall.

How could I still be alive? Yet there I was, somehow hovering above this gory scene. And yet my broken body lying at the foot of the bridge seemed to be the focus of everything.

Surely, I couldn't last for long in such a state? I looked below for help. Both platforms were deserted. Dredging up dark dreams from my difficult childhood, I wondered if I was doomed to look down and watch my life ebbing away. Was this the Hell they'd all talked of so often? I began to recall fragments of those alarming stories I'd heard on Sundays so many years ago.

The next few moments looking down at my unmoving body were the worst I'd experienced, up to that point. I remember having this thought at the time. Perhaps, despite their brevity, they were even worse than anything I was to know later. Then, my World went dark.

*

Gradually, like a jigsaw puzzle being put together, piece by piece, by some unknown hand, I started to become aware of my surroundings once again. As before, I was in the odd, disembodied state, floating somewhere above the footbridge. Looking beneath me, I could still see my prone body lying at the foot of the staircase. Then, all at once, I sensed rather than saw there was someone else on the station.

A flicker of movement near the platform entrance confirmed this impression. In the shadows, I could make out the figure of a tall man. The last train had already left. Whoever it was must have been someone who'd poked his head in for a quick smoke, away from the heavy rain and the fog. Sure enough, a match flared. Soon, the glowing tip of his cigarette danced in the gloom.

As the match ignited, I briefly made out the man's face. It was the greasy haired Jim Corcoran, my fellow passenger of a few minutes before. He wasn't the first person I'd have looked to for help, but what choice did I have?

He stepped forward a pace. I could see he was looking in the opposite direction from where my body was lying, exhaling a cloud of cigarette smoke into the thickening cloud of fog. The centre of this seemed to be hanging a few feet above his head. Curiously, it looked at first as if the fog was emanating from within his lanky body. The man looked like he had not a care in the world. Appearances can sometimes be deceptive, as I was soon to discover.

I, on the other hand, was becoming desperate. Even if he turned his head, he might not have been able to make out my body lying in the shadows at the foot of the bridge. My attempts at shouting brought only silence.

'*Move, you fool! I need help! Walk up the platform!*'

These were my silent thoughts. Suddenly, to my surprise and gratitude, he turned his head and started to amble towards the footbridge.

'Faster, damn you, faster! There can't be much time.'

He accelerated into something more like a sedate walking pace. Finally, he reached the spot where I was lying. I swear tears filled his eyes when he first saw me lying there. Nevertheless, he seemed to have quickly decided there was no hope for me.

'Do something, you idiot! Don't just stand there.'

After gazing down at my body and, believe it or not, crying helplessly for a full minute, he suddenly threw down his cigarette stub with resolution. Then he squinted up and down the lengths of both platforms.

It was clear to me that he was making sure he was alone, and unobserved. Then, he bent down, rolled me over, and carefully felt all over my torso. His hand reached into my right-hand jacket pocket and came out with my wallet.

He stood up and flipped the tatty thing open. Even in the gloom, I could make out the look on his face as his long, hairy fingers came across all the banknotes. It was one that seemed to be of relief rather than anything else. Next, he found the blurred photograph of my mother in youth I always carried, looked at it admiringly, so it seemed to me, and carefully pushed it back inside the wallet.

I knew there was nothing else in the wallet except my crumpled library card. Corcoran found this and contemptuously tore it in pieces, showering the fluttering white fragments onto the railway line. Then he thrust the notes back into the wallet to join the photograph. The wallet he slid into his own trouser pocket, patting it as if to make sure it was safe. I hated this self-congratulatory gesture of his.

Looking in deep thought, or so it seemed to me from my elevation, he glanced up and down both platforms again. Satisfied he was still unwatched, he crouched down next to my body once more. Systematically, he went through each one my jacket pockets. The outside breast pocket was empty, but he took the two shillings and ninepence from the right-hand side, where my wallet had been.

Then his hand dipped into the other side pocket, and he extracted my 'normal' money. This was a handful of loose change, mostly in copper, and a single pound note. He grimaced as he counted the small value of the coins. For a moment, he made as if to scatter them onto the railway line after the pieces of the library card, although soon seemed to think better of it, and pocketed the lot.

Finally, he slid his hand into the inside pocket and pulled out the short letter and envelope he'd given to me not long before. He stood up and read the letter, with visible sadness, for some moments. Then he shredded letter and envelope between his bony fingers, scattering them on the track to join the pieces of my library card.

After this, again seemingly with sudden resolve, he bent over for a third time and started tugging at my shoulders. I was much the smaller of the two of us, but it was still a struggle for him to drag me to the very edge of the platform.

At last, he succeeded in completing his grisly task, and stood erect when my body was precariously balanced. Next, he took out his cigarettes, lit one and took a few puffs before strolling around behind my body. Finally, he put his foot against my shoulder, and gave it a hefty shove. My body tumbled from the platform and onto the track below.

I was horrified. Somewhere, I'd read that falling onto a track didn't necessarily mean you were going be electrocuted. It depended on where exactly you made contact. But my head had flopped like that of a rag doll in my fall. Was I already dead? Corcoran had clearly decided I was.

How could this be if I could still see everything? I'd surely be no longer of this world in any sense after the early morning train from the western end of the line rolled into the station.

Then he looked over the edge of the platform, surveying his handiwork as he smoked his cigarette down to a short butt. While he was smoking, his expression again became one of profound sadness. This was all very well but what about his casual disposal of the body he'd just robbed? Even if he was desperate for money, I couldn't get over the seemingly cool, systematic way in which he'd taken it.

What happened next, I find impossible to describe adequately. The way I still think of it is '*I became a ball of fury*'. This is more or less what did actually happen. My anger generated a strange but entirely real kind of heat and, without consciously thinking about it, I seemed to launch myself down to the spot where Jim Corcoran stood smoking.

[2] Jim

There was a blinding flash. It made me dizzy, and I fell to my knees. For some moments, I was entirely disorientated. Then, gradually, I started to recover my scrambled wits. I rested both hands on my thighs from an awkward, crouched posture – this was the best I could manage – and pushed against them. When I did at last manage to struggle into something like a standing position, I tried to calm myself by drawing in deep gasps of breath.

Slowly, I began to gather my thoughts together more fully. I didn't seem to be hurt in any way. But why should I suddenly be wearing a pair of light blue jeans? I'd never owned a pair of these in my life. Didn't like the colour one bit.

Gingerly, I eased my hands from my knees – at first it really felt as if, unsupported, my legs might not be able to hold me up – and stared disbelievingly at the backs of them. How come they were now hairy, with long, slender fingers ending in phenomenally dirty fingernails? Something was very wrong.

Carefully, I eased myself up to a more normal standing position, my knees creaking more than usual. Glancing over the edge of the platform, I could see a sight that alarmed me even more than when I had seen it from above: there was something that looked like me, slumped as before across the rail next to the nearside platform. There was not the least flicker of life in my form. From this short distance, I could only judge myself to be quite dead.

It's some experience to see your lifeless form on a live electric line, let me tell you. I looked down again and saw on the platform the elongated shadow of this strange me standing there, bemused. I glanced down at my chest and saw I — *he* – was wearing a donkey jacket. Again, this was something I never did. A lock of hair, greasy and now damp from the rain, fell across my cheek. My hands went up to my face. They met with a large, hooked nose.

Jim Corcoran. How...? Somehow, I must have taken possession of his body. He had become me. Or would it be better for me to say I'd become him? I didn't know.

This might be in a new body I somehow found myself in but, in the strained act of rising, I'd already had plenty of demonstration that, although taller, this frame was less efficient than the one I was used to. Otherwise, I still felt every bit myself. I'd retained my own thoughts, memories, and desires. There was no trace of Corcoran's own.

At this moment, my overwhelming desire was to get far away from this platform. As soon as I'd managed to get my thoughts in some sort of order, I made my uncertain way towards the exit, despite the grim knowledge of what was behind me on the track.

I supposed I'd have to find a way to get used to the idea of what had happened to me, even if I couldn't begin to understand it. What choice did I have? But, just before I reached the entrance hall, I grew more uneasy. It was my body on the line, after all. Or at least, it was what my body had now become.

Old Jack, I knew, never locked up the station until twenty-five minutes after the last train had gone. That should give me another ten minutes or so.

I should at least say something to Jack about what had happened, even though I'd have to try to make what I said sound like a believable story. I could simply tell him Steve Charles had fallen accidentally. This was what had happened, after all. Naturally, he'd want to call the police. This meant I'd have to tell them the same story, although I'd have to say a lot more. It worried me, this thought of the police.

I didn't have a clue as to what I was going to say to the law without sounding like a madman, but it might be the only thing for me to do. Clear it all up, sort of thing. Perhaps this might save a few awkward questions later?

Old Jack was someone I'd counted as a friend for years, even when I was still in the children's home. When I had enough money, I'd always travel over to travel over to North Ruislip. What I wanted to do was just walk around the place I couldn't help thinking of as home…

But wait a minute. Did Jack even know Jim Corcoran? As I came into the entrance hall, I was still trying to work out what would be the best way to greet him. It would have to be as Jim, of course.

When I stepped into the small entrance hall, there was no sign of Jack or of anyone else. Strange: all the lights were still on, and the gate was wide open. This meant Jack hadn't yet closed the station. Anyway, he knew I was always on the last train on a Wednesday night.

OK, so a recognisable Steve Charles wouldn't be walking out tonight – at least in his own body – but the old guy must have seen Jim Corcoran going back in for a smoke earlier. Jack surely knew Jim was still in the station. So, where on Earth could Jack have gone?

I waited until after the time the station was normally locked up. Jack must have had to leave early, in a hurry for some reason. But for him to leave the station unattended – it didn't make sense. After another five minutes, there was still no sign of the man. No-one else was in sight, so I stepped out onto a silent Station Road. The rain continued to fall, even heavier than before.

Despite this, the fog in the air was growing thicker. This seemed to me to be an unnatural combination. Still, everything about me looked normal, even the half-finished and stunningly awful round tower above the station exit. But, somehow, things still felt far from right. Yet how could I expect anything to feel normal after what had happened to me? My mind was in a state of confusion as I headed off towards my lodgings.

I felt the edges of a single key attached to a large, rounded piece of metal in the pocket of the donkey jacket and drew this out. It was an ordinary Yale key, attached to an elaborate scrolled fob with the legend 'Home Sweet Home' and heavily embossed with the ornate numbers one and two.

My own key – the key to Steve's front door – was in one of the pockets of the jacket worn by the corpse. This was still lying on the railway track alongside one of the platforms of North Ruislip Underground station.

Wait a minute – it should be *Jim*'s lodgings I was heading for, shouldn't it? I remembered the address from the letter in the other pocket of this jacket – 12, Cypress Close. This was no further to reach from the station than my own lodgings, I knew, but this smelly donkey jacket I now wore was already drenched through. Raindrops were streaming from my hair and down my face long before I reached my destination.

Standing on the doorstep of number twelve, all I could think of doing was getting inside and to give myself a good towelling down. The road looked in every way like my own – medium-sized white houses built between the wars, all as silent as if they were uninhabited.

Still, most of North Ruislip was like this. Even though I had the key, I stood motionless, looking at it dumbly as I grasped the metal awkwardly in a hand unfamiliar to me. It felt as if I was on the point of doing a break-in.

*

Although my fingers were trembling, the key turned easily in the lock. Nervously, I edged the door open.

'Jim. That you?' It was a woman's voice.

The owner of the voice put her head around the first doorway on the right. Lights from a TV screen flickered in the interior behind her, but the sound of the set was muted. Draped across her arm was a fluffy, yellow towel.

It looked warm and inviting, as if she'd somehow sensed my greatest wish. She was a fat, unbecoming woman and looked to be well into her sixties. When I'd first heard her voice, I was expecting no raving beauty, but she was a very long way from being one. The left side of her face was puffed up in an extraordinary way.

'Here Lover,' she said, tossing the huge towel to me. 'You know I'd like to give you a rub-down myself but, to tell you the truth, I'm not at my best tonight. I've spent most of the afternoon with Butcher Bill, the dentist.'

That would explain her puffy face, then. I smiled.

'So, if you wouldn't mind, Jim, we'll have to miss out on our little arrangement for tonight. I'll have to sleep in my own room. I'm sure I'll be fine for you tomorrow. If not, don't worry about the rent. Maybe we'll have two nights next week, eh?' She smiled and looked hopeful.

I was alarmed. Jim's unorthodox rent arrangements sounded scary to me.

'You all right yourself, Lover? Best get your own head on the pillow early. It's a filthy night out there and you seem to have brought the worst of it in with you.'

'It might be a good idea at that.' Was that harsh rasping sound my new voice? The tongue felt awkward in this mouth. The mouth itself felt cavernous and tasted too much of tobacco. 'I'll turn in straight away now, Mrs... Mrs...' I had no idea of what to call her.

She tipped back her head and laughed uproariously.

'Mrs? That's a good one. You never call me that, especially on a Wednesday night! I thought the names of one of the animals in the farmyard would be more to your taste tonight. You know Jim, I do like the things you call me. I love all the things you do, too. Especially on a Wednesday...

'You enjoy the names and noises part of it best, don't you? Our farmyard game is fun for us both, but you know my favourite of all has to be when you do the sprint finish at the Olympics. Ooo, I do *adore* that.' Her face creased into a horrifying smile. 'Well, the thought of that little pleasure has cheered me up no end. Maybe, after all, we could –'

'No!' I couldn't stop the unfamiliar voice from almost shouting this out.

'Well, perhaps you are right at that,' she said. 'You're not looking quite A1 yourself tonight. You're bit pasty as well as wet through, I'd say. But maybe we could look forward to tomorrow, couldn't we? Anyway, before you climb a single stair, I'm going to put that towel to good use.'

Saying this, she strode forward and snatched the towel from my hands. Vigorously, she dried my hair. Almost before I knew it, she'd taken off my donkey jacket, had three buttons of my shirt undone, and had unloosed my belt. I was stunned. Carelessly, she pressed her huge bosom against me.

'It's all right,' I said, a little too quickly. 'I can take care of everything.'

'You are a one. Well, go on then.'

She stood back and watched with wry amusement as I tried awkwardly to dry myself. I have to admit my towelling was much less efficient than hers. Eventually, I finished my task, after some sort of fashion. The towel was still in my hand. What should I do with it?

'You haven't so much as touched your shoulders or your legs. Or your old man.' She laughed again and made a grab between my legs. She was amused by my flinch. 'I have seen it plenty of times before, you know. Is it drooping after being out so long in all that rain?

'Maybe the droop is why you're so shy tonight? Well then, you'd better take the towel up with you. Make sure you use it thoroughly this time. Hang it on the radiator when you're finished with it. I'll see to everything in the morning.' She winked. 'Perhaps I'll see to you, too.'

I didn't trust myself to answer and hurried up the stairs before she could say anything else.

When I reached the top of the staircase, I saw four doors on the small landing. None of these was even slightly ajar and I wondered which led to the bathroom. I'd soon be needing that. But, more immediately, behind which of the doors was what was supposed to be my room? I had no clue, so stepped forward and opened one of the doors in the middle.

This revealed a room with flowered wallpaper, rose-embroidered curtains and a large bed covered by a pink eiderdown. There was a dressing table laid out carefully with a hairbrush, comb, and a number of bottles.

An overpowering smell of talcum powder hit me with my first breath, and I stepped back, turning away involuntarily. My eyes met with those of the woman. She had silently followed me up the stairs.

'No Jim,' she said firmly. 'You know I never do it in here. Off-limits, my own room is. I'll come in there with you now if you like.' With her thumb she indicated the door on the left of her own. 'I'm feeling so much perkier, thanks to you.'

I'm not sure if it was the smell of all that powder or the thought of what she'd just said. It was probably both, but my hands involuntarily went up to my neck.

'Bad throat, is it? I'm not surprised, after being out in that storm. Never mind, Jim. You get yourself into bed just as soon as you've dried yourself down properly. Naughty Flo will have to wait until the morning for her little treat. We'll do anything you like. Farmyard games if you want.'

'Night Flo,' I said. She'd told me which door to open and given me her name.

*

The room – my bedroom – couldn't have been more unlike Flo's pink chamber. There was a chunky wardrobe filling a full quarter of the floor space. It looked as if it dated from well before the First World War.

Against the opposite wall was a plain dressing table, nothing like as graceful as the one in Flo's room. This was wedged in tightly beneath the small window. The furnishings were completed by a largish, lumpy looking bed in the centre. Next to this stood a wobbly bedside cabinet. And that was it.

So, this was where I would be living my new life, was it? What about this new body I'd suddenly inherited? I stood in front of the dressing-table mirror and stripped off my sodden clothing. Jim Corcoran was lanky and thin, rather than tall and slim.

He had been, I suppose, not much more than a year or two above his mid-forties. Clearly, though, he hadn't been looking after himself. There were a number of discolorations pock-marking his body. Despite the general scantiness of build, a potbelly was its prominent feature. I looked down at his – my – dangling penis. '*You poor bastard; that'll teach you not to pay your rent,'* I reflected.

As I had this thought, I quickly looked around to see if there was a bolt on the bedroom door I could pull. There wasn't, so I opened all the drawers on the dresser, searching them one-by-one until I'd found a reasonably intact pair of underpants among the sparse collection of clothing they contained. I felt safer wearing those.

I did a quick inventory of all the clothes I could find while I was looking for the pants. There were three more pairs, all white, two ancient pairs of socks, two worn-looking tee-shirts and a threadbare jersey. I switched my attention to the wardrobe. Hanging there limply on bent wire hangers were two creased long-sleeved shirts and a single pair of denims. With the crumpled, wet heap now strewn on the floor, I'd just viewed the totality of Jim's clothing. He was poorer than me.

Or should I say I had suddenly become even poorer? Besides poverty, I had also gained more than twenty years in age and exchanged my reasonable, if small scale, room for one that had been left to deteriorate.

There was a tarnished sporting cup of some description on the top of the dressing table. Next to this was a three-quarters-empty bottle of cider and I wondered if this was part of the source of Jim's decline. This bottle, and an old-looking scrapbook affair on the top of the dressing table looked like being the sum of Jim's chattels.

Not much of a life, but better than being dead, I suppose. This was the way I'd have to get used to thinking of my old, Steve Charles self. Then I remembered the money I – he – had won at cards earlier in the evening.

I bent down stiffly and took out what had been Jim Corcoran's wallet and all the loose change from the pockets. With the paltry seven shillings and sixpence of Jim's, I had getting on for forty-six pounds. This was the most I'd owned in my life. This thought lifted my confused spirits slightly, although not by much.

'Don't keep that light on all night!' The sudden rap on the door startled me. 'You get your head down for a good sleep. I'll be in for our lovely games in the morning. Maybe we could fit in a sprint finish as well. We both enjoy that. Ooo, I'm so looking forward to it.'

As soon as Flo had gone from outside the door, a growing pressure on my bladder reminded me of my neglect to urinate before I came into the bedroom.

I was afraid to go to the bathroom – I could picture an alarming encounter on the dark landing – so I resolved to wait at least fifteen minutes before opening the door, hoping to pick the right one of the two remaining doors. But, as always in these situations, sitting at the foot of the bed and doing nothing made me all the more aware of my bodily discomfort.

I looked around for some distraction. On the dressing-table top were only the bottle, without any kind of accompanying drinking container, and the scrapbook. For a moment I confess I thought of the cider. It was a drink I'd never cared for, yet my tongue curled in my mouth. I even felt myself beginning to salivate.

There must still have been some trace of Jim left in this body, even if only at the most basic physical level. How would I react to Flo's presence in the morning? I shuddered at the thought and picked up the sporting trophy to examine it.

It clearly hadn't been polished for a very long time. All the same, I could see this was no second-rate award. Unkindly, I thought that the prize must have meant a lot to Jim, otherwise he'd have pawned it. I looked at the engraved lettering: '*Saturday, 19th June 1937: To James Corcoran, our future World Record Holder, for his star performances in the County of Middlesex Athletics Championships, most particularly for running a mile in the winning time of 4:07:52.*'

If the cup had told me he'd received his award for charity work, I couldn't have been more surprised. Jim Corcoran an athlete! When I thought of the sad sight greeting me in the mirror a few minutes ago I wondered for a moment if this could be the same person.

Under four minutes and eight seconds was serious stuff in 1937, too. I'd been out of school for only a year or two when Roger Bannister sent the country into hysterics by running the first sub four-minute mile. Jim had won his cup nearly seventeen years earlier.

Fascinated, I picked up the scrapbook. I wanted to know more about the man whose body I'd taken over. The first four pages were taken up by press cuttings from our local paper, *The West Middlesex Gazette*. All of them featured the achievements of Jim Corcoran on the track in 1937 and the first half of 1938.

There were so many reports of an athlete of great promise. On the scrapbook's back cover were also pasted two photographs, clearly snipped from the same source as the reports. The newsprint was blurred and beginning to yellow with age but good enough to show the lean, yet wiry, athletic build Jim possessed back then.

On the scrapbook's seventh page, all by itself, was a brief cutting from a newspaper article dated 18th February 1938. Its headline was *A Mile in Under Four Minutes?* The writer was someone by the name of Duncan Goodley. I read:

'Your reporter has only just emerged from a detailed interview with Dr Henry Carter. Readers may not be familiar with this name, but Dr Carter is the trainer, mentor, and all-round inspiration for Solicitor's Clerk James Corcoran, better known as North Ruislip's fast-rising athletic phenomenon.

'Since Dr Carter took the young man under his wing in the autumn of 1936, Mr Corcoran has most certainly been the one to watch as he breezes around running tracks, seemingly without much effort. His best (unofficial) time recorded over a mile is 4:06:05, a mere one-sixtieth of a second behind the current World record. This was achieved in training last August. Dr Carter is confident this time will be easily bettered by Mr Corcoran this year.

'He adds that his athlete's ultimate target is the 1940 Olympic Games, scheduled for Tokyo but likely to be relocated to Helsinki because of the turmoil of the new Sino-Japanese War, which broke out last year. Wherever the games are held, says Dr Carter, he is quite sure Corcoran will be bringing back both a gold medal and a new World record for the mile in under four minutes. He also feels Corcoran will still be young enough be able to defend his gold medal on home soil when the Games come to London in 1944.

'Time alone will tell whether or not these bold claims, particularly that of achieving a sub four-minute mile, are realistic. However, there can be no doubt that Corcoran is an exciting middle-distance runner, and your Gazette will continue to bring you reports of his progress towards this goal.'

Upon the opposite page was pasted a letter, written untidily on a single sheet of paper, and signed 'Harry' – presumably, Dr Carter. No sender's address was given, and the only date given was a scribbled 'May 1938'. I read:

'Jim – In haste – I was amazed to get your letter this morning. You are right: The World is in an utter mess and the international situation is becoming worse day by day. The things that *might happen could indeed have a harmful effect on our sport, precisely as you say. But we don't know any of the details for sure. I shouldn't worry too much about the Germans marching their troops into Austria last March. I can understand your worries but most probably that is where it will end. We should rely on Mr Chamberlain and his people to do the right thing for our country. None of us wants another war after the last. As you know, I fought in France and Belgium myself in that great conflict.*

'I was surprised to read your news about M and the baby coming to her in November. I'd have thought this would make you want to stay at home with your girl – or even want to marry her – rather than rushing off to join the army to 'make the world safe for my family' as you put it.

'You'd be better off by far to stay put in that solicitor's office to wait and see what will happen. Please don't do anything rash before you've spoken to me. I have to go to Birmingham this morning, but I'll be back on Thursday and promise to call around to see you just as soon as I return. We really do need to talk about this.'

It seemed to me that, despite what Henry Carter had said, Jim must have thrown everything up to join the army. How romantically misguided of him. What had happened after this? We all knew what had happened to the World. Jim had been more perceptive than this Dr Carter in his view of the future, if not in what he chose to do about it.

But what happened to Jim in later years? I turned the page of the scrapbook. There was only one further entry. This was pencilled directly on the page in a small, neat hand. It was undated but gave every appearance of having been added very recently:

'What am I to do? The Pethwick Gang are saying that if I don't pay the two hundred quid they say I owe them by the end of November I'm going to get it. We all know what that means: lights out time. I don't owe them this much money at all. It's nearer to a ton.

Anyway, it makes no difference. I don't have the faintest hope of getting either amount together. I suppose, if I could put my hands on forty or fifty quid, I could scrape together another fifty or so with Flo's help. But I dread to ask her. She'd want me to marry her for that kind of money. She's been making noises about us tying the knot for months now. Marry Flo! I'd rather tie a knot in my neck. But this is exactly what the Pethwicks would do to me.'

Poor Jim. What a mess he was in. No wonder he'd been so pleased to find the contents of my wallet.

It seemed wrong to leave the scrapbook – all that was left from Jim's own life, really – lying casually around, so I opened the empty bottom drawer of the dressing table to put it out of sight.

The drawer wasn't as empty as I'd first thought. When I'd looked before, in my haste I'd missed the small, grubby cloth bag lying on the bottom. I picked this up and found inside two fading photographs, together with a small piece of notepaper, obviously torn roughly out of a notebook.

The pictures were of the obverse and reverse sides of a Victoria Cross medal. The latter was badly out-of-focus but the engraving on the suspension bar showed clearly that the medal had been awarded to James Corcoran.

There was little written on the piece of paper, just a cryptic scrawl in the same tiny handwriting as the longer note I'd just read:

'FOR VALOUR? I don't think so. I don't deserve this. Anyway, the Pethwicks want their Christmas present, so we'll see what I get for this bit of tin they gave me for Dunkirk.'

So, Jim had won a medal and had to sell it through fear of this Pethwick Gang, whoever they were. He was hardly my idea of a hero. Nor was he his own, going by what he'd written.

There was no time to wonder further. I couldn't wait another moment before easing my bladder, so I quietly switched off the bedroom light and stepped as silently as I could manage onto the dark landing. I dared not switch on its light for fear of alerting Flo.

There was a nervous moment on the landing when I couldn't remember for certain which of the doors led to Flo's bedroom and which I thought would be that to the bathroom. Fortunately, I chose the right one and thoroughly, and as silently as I could in the darkness, let my urine go in a torrent. I could have shouted out with relief. Then I tip-toed back to my bed, pulled the counterpane around my ears, and was asleep within minutes.

*

The first half-light of morning was entering my room as a loud noise wrenched me from my sleep, shattering a complex dream with me on a running track, cheered on all sides by a large crowd, every one of them with the faces of Jim's landlady. Harsh salvos of rapping on the door knocker formed the first sounds my bleary wakefulness met. Several more knocks followed before I heard Flo clumping down the stairs while grumbling softly to herself.

I heard the front door being opened and the muffled sounds of three voices. One belonged to Flo. Its tone was at first indignant. The other two were male and told of more patience, at least to begin with. As the conversation went on, the other voices also became more strident. Finally, I heard the front door being closed and a series of heavy footsteps coming up the stairs.

Fully awake now, I sat up in bed and fixed my gaze on the door. After a tense second of silence, the door opened. Two men, one wearing a gabardine mac and a trilby, the taller man a police uniform, strode in. There wasn't space in the room for Flo and she waited anxiously in the doorway.

'James Corcoran?' said the shorter man, obviously some sort of detective.

'Uh?' I suppose I was, in a way at least, although hearing myself addressed like this threw me and I couldn't answer properly.

'Get yourself out of that bed, sunshine,' he said. 'You're in really big trouble this time.'

'Detective Sergeant Williams, I've already told you.' This was Flo's forlorn voice from the doorway. 'He's been with me all day. I swear to you.'

This Williams man turned his head towards Flo. He addressed her gently.

'Now, Mrs Stocker. Please don't get yourself involved in this. I'll ignore what you just said. This is a profoundly serious matter. My mum was in school with you, back in the old days. She'd never forgive me if I had to arrest you while I was here.

'Anyway, Constable George and I know exactly where Corcoran was all day yesterday. In the afternoon he was involved in his usual shady business in Parva-vale. We've got a number of witnesses who've already made sworn statements to that effect.'

Then he turned to me. His lip curled and his voice hardened.

'We know where you were late last night, especially, my lad. We've got you bang to rights. Now, get your clothes on. You're coming down to the station with us.'

Weren't they supposed to give me some sort of formal warning? Detective Sergeant

Williams hadn't even told me what the charge was. But I could guess.

*

It's been closed for years now, but in those days North Ruislip Police Station was housed in an undistinguished, poky building thrown up in hasty response to the suburb's rapid growth during the nineteen-twenties. The tiny room we were in was windowless, lit from above by a single bulb adorned with a plain, brown shade. This robbed it of most of its weak power of illumination.

Sitting opposite me at the plain bench, the only piece of furniture except for the four chairs around it were Detective Sergeant Williams and a Detective Inspector Young. The latter had been brought in, so he'd informed me, because this was supposed to be a 'big' case. I'd already been here for at least an hour.

I was getting confused and could see they were becoming more exasperated by the minute with what I was trying to tell them. At the same rate I was getting more nervous because I was expecting Williams to walk around to my side of the table again and apply more of what he called 'persuasion'. He'd already given me a few preliminary samples of this.

'Now, let's get your story straight,' said Young. 'You think carefully before you answer this time, Jim. Got that? So, what you're trying to say is that Steve Charles died as the result of an accident. He fell from the top of the steps. Is that how it was?'

'Yes, sir. That's exactly what happened.'

'And you want to go on saying you had nothing at all to do with it?'

He looked at me as if I was some species of moron.

'Well, it was my foot that must have slipped on the wet step. Like, I keep trying to explain, I'm really Steve...'

My voice tailed off as the two policemen exchanged glances.

'So,' said Young. 'You still want to say you're actually Steve Charles. Are you quite sure about this?'

'Yes. I am.'

'You still want to persist with this silly story, even though Mrs Florence Stocker has clearly identified you as James Corcoran, her lodger for the last eighteen months? And where were you – sorry, where was Jim – after young Steve took his tumble?'

'I don't know. Somewhere outside having a smoke, I think.'

'You THINK?' The two men exchanged broad smiles. 'And yet you admit that you – sorry, Jim – systematically went through Steve Charles's pockets and took out around forty-five pounds.'

He rolled his eyes theatrically.

'We know from enquiries they made from the local station that young Mr Charles won this money at a card game in Parva-vale earlier tonight. Wonderful thing, the telephone. I'll make a wager with you. Most of that money – a decent sum, you'll agree – will be in your wallet in this very room right at this moment. That the wallet there? The one with the initials SC on it?'

'Yes,' I said. 'That's my wallet. I bought it in Southend a few years ago. It's the only time in my life I've been to the seaside…'

It sounded so lame, even though it was the truth. Young smiled again and looked at Williams.

'Never mind all that nonsense for now,' he said. 'Did you, the person in front of me – forget for a moment what you think your name is, put the wallet on the bedside cabinet earlier? Or do you want to say someone else came in and put the wallet there for you? The tooth fairy, perhaps?'

'Well,' I said. 'In a manner of speaking it was me who put it there.'

Young glowered.

'For goodness' sake. Can you show me which hand put it there? Was it Flo's hand, perhaps? You hold the hand that put it there up for me, there's a good chappie.'

Standing on the threshold of the room, Flo stiffened. Her expression became one of alarm. She caught my glance and shook her head.

'No, of course it wasn't this lady. This was the hand.'

I held up my right hand.

'Higher!'

Nervously, I put the hand right up. Williams, standing beside Young, almost had a fit of giggles.

'At last. Now we're beginning to get somewhere. Take a look inside that wallet, Williams. Show all of us – Corcoran especially – exactly what you find inside.'

Williams stepped over and picked up the wallet. Carefully and very deliberately, he took each one of the notes from it and displayed them one at a time to his audience of three. He was like a stage conjurer performing a magic trick. All the time he wore a self-satisfied grin.

'Would you like to explain how this money found its way into your possession?' Young was smiling too, now.

'Jim Corcoran – before I took his body over – took all my money and my wallet and then flung my body on the railway line.'

'Ah,' said Young. 'We agree on something, then. So, tell me this. If you weren't Jim at that time and Steve was lying dead as a doornail on the platform, how did you see all this?'

'My spirit – my essence, or whatever you want to call it – was floating above the platform.'

'I've had enough of this rubbish,' said Young, looking at the Sergeant. 'Haven't you?'

'Shall I give him a proper flip this time, Sir?

'No need to waste your time, Detective Sergeant.' Williams looked disappointed. 'We need to bring this to an end, or we'll be listening to this gibberish until it's time for lunch.'

He faced me, a sardonic smile on his lips.

'Look Jim. We've humoured you for long enough. We've got a signed statement from Jack Marchant at the tube station. Look, they're trying out this new experimental system at North Ruislip. They've got a few television cameras set up to give views on a TV screen back in the ticket office. Jack saw most of what you did tonight. We have it all in a formal written statement. You may as well make a sensible confession.'

A flash of hope came to me.

'If Jack was watching me, he'll know that I – Jim – didn't kill anyone. He'll have seen Steve Charles falling from the bridge. If he says anything different… Old Jack's a liar.'

I felt so uncomfortable saying this.

'See?' The Inspector turned to the Sergeant. 'Those cameras won't be any real use until they start using a workable way of recording the pictures. You know, like music on tape recorders. They could do it now if they want to, from what I hear. Then we could run through the tapes for every second of the day without having to rely on when someone happened to be looking at a TV screen.'

He tossed his head in indignation.

'Old Jack, Corcoran calls him, does he?' He smiled at Williams. 'Bit familiar, wouldn't you say, Detective Sergeant Williams? Jack Marchant doesn't know Our Jim, except by sight. Says he's a surly bastard. Never speaks to anyone, that one, he says.

'The pillock doesn't seem to realise that no court in the World would take the word of a small-time crook before that of an upstanding citizen. Besides, Jack knew poor Steve Charles well. Used to see the lad going home every Wednesday night when he was working a late shift at the station, so he told us. The poor man was in tears when he told us how Corcoran must have killed Steve.'

Something didn't add up. Old Jack would never make up a story like this, let alone put his signature to it.

'But Steve's death was an accident, I keep telling you. Jim was somewhere outside when he fell. He was nowhere near Steve. Mr Marchant wasn't even in the ticket office when I left.'

Inspector Young turned to me again, a look of disgust on his face.

'Which "I" are we talking about now, eh? The Steve Charles "I" or the Jim Corcoran "I"? Jack Marchant was in the ticket office when you passed for the second time. He was trying to hide down behind the counter. You didn't expect him to sit and wait for the same treatment from the Jim "I", did you? As soon as he thought you were safely out of the way he called 999.'

He shook his head in mock sorrow.

'Haven't you worked it out yet? That's how come Detective Sergeant Williams here was able to pick you up so quickly. We'd have got you straight away if Jack knew your name properly or where you lived. As things were, he was able to tell us where Steve had been tonight – Parvavale – and the boys at the local station were able to move quickly. Police Officers aren't really plods, you know, despite what your sort thinks.'

'But–'

'But nothing,' he said. 'Jack didn't say he actually saw you push Steve from the bridge. He couldn't have; he was carrying out another duty at the time. But he did look at the TV monitor a few minutes later. He told us he was surprised when Steve hadn't come out by that time. That's what made him look.

'This was when he saw you, Corcoran. You were going through the pockets of the deceased. Jack was crying when he told us the way you hoofed the boy's body from the platform onto the line. Bastard.

'If Jack hadn't seen you doing this, Steve's corpse would have still been there when the first train came through this morning. It would have been handy for you when the train mangled the lad's body. That was your plan, Corcoran, wasn't it?'

Young's eyes narrowed. For a moment I thought he was going to come around to my side of the table and punch me himself, rather than letting Williams do it once again.

'The Underground people have already checked the ticket records for us. They confirm what Jack said. The two of you would have been the only passengers left on the train when it reached North Ruislip. You both got off there. Old Jack has given us a sworn statement to say that no one else beside you came out straight after the train stopped. Who else could have killed Steve Charles?'

Jim Corcoran must have gone out to the street, seen how much it was raining, and decided to come back in to have his smoke. This was why he hadn't seen me – Steve – fall from the footbridge. It was why Jack had seen him passing twice. But I didn't trust myself to give a sensible explanation of this. I held my silence.

'Right, Detective Sergeant. This is what we do. You go out there and type up a statement for Mr Corcoran to sign. You know what to say. You don't have to go over the top about the push from the bridge. Just say there was a struggle for Steve Charles' wallet, and the boy fell.'

He laughed grimly.

'You can even say that Mr Corcoran claimed he didn't intend to throw him off the bridge. I'll stay here for another ten minutes and try to make this gentleman understand that it'd make it easier for everyone if he signed the statement without making any more fuss. Send that young Constable George in to see I don't put unfair pressure on the accused, would you?'

Young winked at Williams. They both laughed. Then Williams suddenly stopped laughing.

'You want me to write it exactly like that, Inspector?' The junior policeman looked puzzled. 'Won't it look like Corcoran is claiming Charles' death was an accident?'

'Fat lot of notice the jury will take of a story of that kind, Detective Sergeant Williams.'

They both laughed again.

*

'I think I've written down everything you've told me this time. You, as Steve Charles, the victim, travelled from Parva-vale to North Ruislip on the same train as James Corcoran. You'd told your solicitor, Mr Barlow, that you'd seen Corcoran often of late because his lodgings were near to yours, but the two of you had never before exchanged a word before the night of 25th November 1959. And you've now taken over his body. Do I have your story right at last?'

The person Barlow, or his chambers' clerk, had appointed as my barrister was now facing me across a small table. He'd told me he'd had to get special legal approval to speak to me directly, without Barlow being present, considering this to be necessary after what my solicitor had said to him.

He was a young man – he seemed to be younger than me – Steve –, though I suppose he couldn't have been. His nose was thin and bony. He had uncannily bright eyes. This man had introduced himself as Mr Talbot. I never found out what his first name was.

'Yes, I've told you all this three times. Jim Corcoran only said a few words to me on the train.'

For a long minute he looked down at his papers, saying nothing.

'And you are quite sure you want to stick to every detail of this story, Mr Corcoran?'

'It's the truth. And my name is Steve Charles, not Jim Corcoran.'

I'd become so confused in the police station and now here in the prison, that the truth was I'd hardly even been certain of my real name.

He sighed theatrically.

'My brief is to act in the capacity of defence counsel to Mr James Corcoran, so I'd prefer to address you by that name if you wouldn't mind. How do you think a jury is going to look upon your story?'

'It's not a story. It's the truth. Do you want me to tell lies?'

Another dramatic pause from him before he spoke.

'I won't ask you to tell an untruth, Mr Corcoran.' Those bright eyes fixed me with an earnest stare. 'As I've said, it seems to me that our best course of action would be to enter a plea of insanity. If you do this then you can stick to your story. Sorry, let me rephrase that – repeat the facts as you see them. In this way, we shouldn't have too much difficulty in establishing that the balance of your mind was disturbed when the crime was committed.'

He hoisted his shiny briefcase onto the table and started to shuffle his papers together. It was clear Talbot was grateful that this interview was coming to an end – to Talbot, it was coming to an end. This case was a big one for him – perhaps his biggest yet – but it was clear he wanted the whole thing to draw to an end quickly.

'There is one other thing,' I said.

'Yes?' Talbot paused midway through the action of replacing the sheaf of papers into his case.

'The police should find something in Jim's room,' I said. 'There's his scrapbook and a few other bits and pieces. A lot of it is made up of old press cuttings – he was an athlete of promise before the war. Some of it though, is his own account. There's one newish entry in there, made by Jim himself. His life was being threatened by some people called the Pethwick gang. There's no need for you to think of an insanity claim. It's simply not true.'

Talbot looked at me carefully before answering in a tone I thought was deliberately condescending.

'Yes. Well, don't get yourself too excited about this.' Talbot resumed the packing of his briefcase. 'The police may not know who this gang may be, but your solicitor tells me they've found the book you're talking about. May I point out to you that this death threat would give you a strong motive for killing and robbing Steve Charles? Think about it for yourself.'

He smiled.

'So, the solicitor has already advised them that, if they produced this book in evidence, we'd have to draw attention to the earlier entries about your sporting achievements. I've read everything in the book for myself.

'This I would have done in any event, of course, in the process of illustrating your status as a brave man, joining the army at an early stage as you seem to have done. I'm trying to make the best case for your defence I can, don't you see that? Not easy in the circumstances.'

A thought came to me.

'What about the medal? Jim's Victoria Cross?'

He looked surprised.

'What medal? The solicitor said nothing about a medal.'

'There was no actual medal. Jim had sold it. But he had photographs.'

'Nothing was said about any photographs, apart from the newspaper cuttings.'

'They could be crucial!'

Talbot sighed.

'Look, I'm telling you your best bet would be to enter a plea of insanity. If you won't let me do that, I'll have to construct the best defence I can. If there's a war medal anywhere, there'll be records. I'll be the one to decide, in consultation with your solicitor, whether this is a matter worthy of investigation. I am counsel for the defence, you know.'

I felt like reaching across the table and grabbing him by the throat. But what would be the point? Talbot took my silence as acquiescence.

'Look, the police have already come to a gentleman's agreement with us that this notebook wouldn't be produced at the trial by either party in evidence. They'll talk about motives unknown for the killing. Don't you see that's the most favourable outcome we could wish to have?

'How can you have a gentleman's agreement about the truth? It seems to me –'

But Talbot was now in pompous full flow.

'However, there can be no denying the presence of Mr Charles's wallet on your dressing table, Mr Corcoran, nor that it contained a lot of money. That money was the money won at cards earlier on the evening of 25th November by Mr Charles.'

He looked at me as if he was dealing with an idiot.

'Don't you see? The police will make sure they have sworn statements to that effect from all four of the others who were present at the game. You can count on it.'

'You do understand that Jim Corcoran won the highest medal in the war? Surely that must count for something? I can't give you any details, but it might be worth you finding out what you can. As you said, there'll be records.'

Talbot smirked when I said this. He actually smirked.

'Oh, come on. I'm sure you know a great deal more than I can ever find out about your war experiences, Mr Corcoran. But I have the definite feeling that it wouldn't be a clever idea to try to make too much of this in court. Your moment of glory was nearly twenty years ago, after all. I believe you served in Belgium later in the war, although with no great distinction, as I understand it.'

There was little I could say. I didn't know any more about Jim Corcoran's war record than did Talbot. In fact, I precisely knew nothing except that Corcoran himself was not proud of it.

'Can you tell me-'

'Mr Corcoran, I really do have to go now. I'll be back tomorrow. That will be my final visit before your trial. Meanwhile, I should recommend that you think very carefully about the advantages of an insanity plea. Some judges don't seem to mind them, even if they are anathema to others. I believe the judge who'll preside at your trial is one of those who considers himself to be more modern-minded than many. We'll find out if this is so.'

*

The court hearing itself was a disaster. Despite my refusal to enter a formal plea of insanity, Talbot still tried to lead the defence that way. Much of the evidence was far too technical for me, but as far as I could see, many of the arguments seemed to be about the nature of insanity and whether it was possible for someone to lose his mind temporarily and then recover it unaided so completely.

Roderick, the sharp lawyer who was prosecuting counsel, had me examined by a doctor. This man, with his gravelly voice, had no trouble convincing the jury I was entirely sane. My confusion about my identity was a mere distasteful pose, he said. My expressed lack of knowledge about Jim's early life, or indeed any part of his life before the night at North Ruislip Station, was an even more cynical one.

My defence counsel was even more inept than I feared he'd be.

There were three moments in the trial that stand out in my mind. The first came on the morning of the second day, when Al from the wallpaper factory appeared as a witness for the prosecution and confirmed that I – Steve Charles, I'm talking about – had won over forty pounds at cards on the night of 25th November. I was livid when he said I'd won it by cheating.

Al admitted he'd tried to follow Steve to Parva-vale tube station, but, so he said, he'd soon lost him. Jim Corcoran – Al knew him from way back, during the war, he claimed – was on his way to the station when Al bumped into him.

It seemed Corcoran was often in Parva-vale mid-week. They only had time for a quick word because Jim wanted to catch the last train. Al had told Jim that Steve had the forty quid he'd won dishonestly. '*Hard luck mate. If I see the little sod, I'll get it back for you,*' was what Al told the court had been Jim's response to what he'd told him.

Al then claimed he'd changed his mind while making his way back home and started to think maybe young Steve had simply been lucky. He regretted saying what he had to Jim and was horrified when he found out Jim had been arrested for Steve's murder. This was why he'd come forward to the police.

When I tried to persuade Talbot to get Den or someone else to appear and say there really had been no cheating at cards, he gave me short shrift. It wasn't Steve Charles we were trying to defend, the lawyer said.

On the next day, Jack Marchant from North Ruislip Station appeared. The verdict was probably settled by his evidence. After all, he was the next best thing to an eyewitness the police had. Even if he hadn't been watching the

TV screen at the crucial moment when Steve fell from the bridge, there could be no denying that he'd actually seen Jim throwing the body onto the line a few minutes later. But it was the way in which he gave his evidence that really won the jury over.

His eyes filled up at every mention of the name of Steve Charles and he looked at me – Jim Corcoran, he naturally thought – with pure hatred in his eyes. Why, by the time he stepped down from the box he almost had me believing I was guilty of my own murder. I remember every word of the key part of his evidence:

'Now, Mr Marchant. Have you seen this man before? Do you know him at all?'

Roderick pointed a finger at me in the dock. He was a smooth operator in every way. It was clear there were years of experience behind him. Every so often he'd flick a look of contempt at my man Talbot as if to say. *This is how you* should *be doing it.*

Jack cleared his throat noisily before answering in a low, almost indistinct, tone.

'He gets on or off the train at my station quite often. I see him most weeks when I'm on late shift. I couldn't say I know him.'

I thought Roderick or the judge were going to tell Jack to speak up, but they didn't. Instead, Roderick dropped his own voice and spoke to Jack in an avuncular sort of way.

'Yet you do know his name, don't you?'

Roderick crossed his arms over his chest and looked smug.

'James Corcoran, he is. I asked one of the other passengers, a mate of mine.'

Jack spoke more clearly now.

'Why didn't you ask Mr Corcoran himself?'

Roderick knew the answer he was going to get.

'Because I was sure I wouldn't get an answer.' Jack cast a contemptuous glance in my direction. 'I'd said "Good Morning" or "Good Evening" to him a few times before that night. He'd just looked at me as if I was something the cat brought in. So, one day I asked my mate Fred instead. Fred used to travel to work on the line. He's just gone on the Old Age.'

'Do you remember the exact words you used to this passenger, Fred?'

'Are you sure you want me to repeat what I said here in court?' Jack looked uncomfortable.

'I want you to use the exact words, if you remember them.'

'All right then. I said, "who's that surly bastard?" Sorry for the language in a place like this but you did ask.'

Roderick threw his hands in the air and looked at the jury for a long moment. You'd have sworn Jim Corcoran was on trial for being a miserable git. Counsel paused to let the message sink in and dropped his voice when he continued.

'Now, Mr Marchant, I'm afraid we have to come to the most difficult part. Please try not to upset yourself again. When was the last time you saw Mr Corcoran?

'On 25th November. When the police came around to the station. When he…when he…'

'Just the date, Mr Marchant. How can you be so sure this was the date?'

'Because I've been off work since then. It's my nerves. You see-'

'What I want to do now, Mr Marchant, is very carefully to go through the key events that led to you calling the police, soon after the last train arrived and not long before the time when, in normal circumstances, you'd have gone off duty. That's the time I'm talking about.

Jack nodded.

'Were you expecting to see anyone you knew alighting from the train?'

The expression of sympathy Roderick wore was worthy of an Oscar winner. The judge twitched. This might not have been a leading question, but Roderick asked it with a leading expression on his face.

'I thought I'd see young Stephen Charles, Sir. He always catches the last train of a Wednesday. Plays cards in Parva-vale, regular as clockwork. Don't know why. He doesn't like it, you know.'

'You've answered the question, Mr Marchant.' The judge perked up. 'Whether Mr Charles like or disliked playing cards is not relevant to the case. Those additional remarks are to be struck from the record.'

Roderick smiled gently at Jack.

'Indeed, Mr Marchant. Please confine yourself to answering my questions. Now, I'm sorry to have to ask this but would you like to tell me who it was you saw instead of Mr Charles?'

Jack looked around the courtroom as if Roderick were trying to catch him out. He wasn't. He was simply indulging his courtroom theatrics. Talbot had warned me to expect a full quota of these. This was about the only thing he did get right during the trial.

'Well,' said Jack. 'Like I said, I was expecting to see young Steve Charles. He always caught the last train home from Parva-vale of a Wednesday. I knew he'd gone there as usual because I saw him about seven o'clock that evening catching the down train. I had a few words with him. I always like to have a chat with Little Steve when I see him.'

At the precise moment Jack said 'Little Steve' a single tear rolled down his cheek. Something about the lighting in the courtroom meant that its glistening wetness stood out. At least it did from where I was, in the dock.

It must have looked the same to the jury, too, because there was a low murmur from that quarter. It made the old judge look at them sternly. Nothing could have been better choreographed. There was only one way this trial was going anyway, but any faint hope Jim – I – could have had evaporated at that moment. Roderick pressed on briskly:

'Please just tell me the name of the passenger who actually did emerge?'

'It was HIM!' He pointed at the dock. 'That man over there. Corcoran.'

'What did you think when you saw James Corcoran instead of Stephen Charles?'

'Like I said to the police, I wasn't completely surprised to see him, as such. This Corcoran man sometimes gets a late train himself. But I knew Little Steve was afraid of him – can't blame him for that. I was nervous of him myself.'

I was afraid of Corcoran? What was Jack saying? I hardly knew the man. I started to protest.

'Silence the accused!' ordered the judge. 'You'll get your chance to speak later.'

Roderick folded his arms in front of him again and waited a few moments with carefully assumed patience after my interruption before speaking again.

'And when were your worst fears confirmed, Mr Marchant?'

'Young Steve still didn't come out. Instead, he,' – he pointed at me again, although everyone knew from the way he glared at me it was Jim Corcoran he was talking about – 'ambled out like he didn't have a care in the world and left by the street exit. After only a couple of minutes he wandered back in again, waving his packet of cigarettes about like a flag. He was trying to make me think he was only coming back in for a smoke, you see...'

'No speculation, please, Mr Marchant, if you'd be so kind.' Roderick said. 'The accused came back in from the road, right?'

'Yes Sir. It was raining quite steadily outside. Passengers sometimes come in for a quick ciggie in the entrance hall or on the platform. That's all I thought he was going to do, at first. It's what he wanted me to think, I tell you. I was still hoping for young Steve to come out. I knew he wouldn't want to wait long on a platform with Corcoran on it.'

Jack Marchant bowed his head in sorrow. Roderick imitated his gesture perfectly. Then he looked up dramatically. He held forth his index figure, as if he wanted to let the jury know this was the crux of the matter.

'And we all know that Mr Charles didn't walk out,' said Roderick. 'We know from their evidence that the police brought his dead body out later.' He turned to the jury, nodding sagely. 'Did you actually see the accused lighting his cigarette?'

'No sir. I started to tidy up while I was waiting for the two of them to leave the station. But he was waving that flashy red packet about, as if he wanted me to think he was going to light one. And then, a few minutes later-'

'Go on, Mr Marchant.'

'I thought I heard a noise from the platform. It wasn't loud, but it was like...'

'Please describe only what you thought you heard, not what the noise may have sounded like. After you thought you heard the noise, did you go out to the platform to investigate?'

Jack looked at Roderick wonderingly.

'No, Sir. I did not. I didn't want the same treatment. So, I ran into my office and turned that television and camera contraption back on. I'd already turned it off for the night you see. I thought I was ready to knock off and go home.'

'And what did you see on the TV screen?'

'Well, it took a few minutes to warm up, see. Then I needed to get the camera pointed at platform one. It's a bit slow, see, and perhaps I am, too, so it took me a few minutes before anything came up on the screen.'

'What did you see on the screen? Speak up please, Mr Marchant. We all realise this is hard for you to say.'

Roderick sounded like a man with infinite patience.

'It was that man – Corcoran. He was bent over young Steve and going through his pockets one-by-one. The screen was a bit fuzzy at that distance, but I swear I saw his wicked face light up when he found the wallet.'

Jack looked towards Roderick, as if he wanted another prompt from him. Roderick merely nodded slightly. After a moment, Jack continued to speak.

'I could even see on the small screen there were a good few notes in the wallet he found in the jacket pocket. I watched him while he counted each one of them, Sir. He was as cool and casual about it all as you like. Then he came upon something small. This must have been the library card the police found scattered on the railway line later. I saw that man…'

He looked at me accusingly.

'He tore the card in pieces and flicked them onto the track, as smooth as you like. Then he bent down again and went through all poor

Steve's other pockets. I think the only other thing he found was some small change.'

Jack made no mention of the photograph or the letter. Perhaps the old picture was too small for him to see on the screen. Anyway, I held my silence. I couldn't see what relevance either had, and I didn't want the judge hushing me again.

'Now, Mr Marchant,' said Roderick, puffing out his chest. 'I need to remind you that you are under oath. Are you absolutely sure there can be no question of incorrect identification? Are you certain it was Mr James Corcoran you saw?'

Old Jack puffed himself up, looking affronted.

'I set the camera on close-up. That's something I do know how to do. Besides, about five minutes later, this man Corcoran walked right past me, bold as brass, on his way out again.'

Roderick bowed his head gravely. When he lifted it once more, his expression was one of indignance.

'We'll come to that, Mr Marchant. What did you next see on the television screen? Answer that question for me if you would, please.'

'He … he…'

At this point Old Jack dissolved in a flood of tears. It was as if the prosecuting barrister had pressed a button at exactly the right moment.

'Would you like me to request the judge to order a short adjournment, Mr Marchant?'

The judge made a throaty noise. I suppose this was meant to show sympathy.

'No, no…I'll carry on, Sir. Corcoran pushed young Steve's body…I could see the boy was already dead, Sir… onto the railway line with his foot. It was horrible, horrible. Then he just stood there, calm as can be, looking up and down the platform. Then – this really surprised me, considering the way he'd acted up until then – he seemed to black out or faint and fell on his knees.'

'And what did you do at that point?'

'At first, I was horrified. I couldn't believe what I'd just seen. All I could do was stand there for a few moments. As soon as I'd come to my senses, I picked up my telephone to call the police.

'But then, just as I was starting to dial, I glanced again at the screen, only to see Corcoran strolling up the platform towards the station exit.

He couldn't have fainted off for more than a few moments.'

Jack stole a quick glance in my direction, as if wondering what kind of man was capable of doing such things.

'Well, I was frightened out of my wits when I realised that thug was heading my way, so I quickly put the telephone back on the receiver and crouched down to hide behind the counter. He walked past me and onto the street, cool as a cucumber. Thank goodness he didn't spot me.'

Roderick, the jury, and most of the others in the court, even the judge, looked indulgently towards the witness box at this point.

'You'd have sworn nothing out of the ordinary had happened. There was a moment when I thought he'd seen me hiding. There was hardly any room for me to conceal myself, do you see? But thank goodness, he hadn't noticed me. I waited a few minutes to make sure he'd gone right away from the station and then I called the police.'

Roderick drew himself up to his full lanky height.

'One further question if I may, Mr Marchant, if only to save my learned friend the trouble of asking it. The last train left North Ruislip station at precisely 11:41pm – we've checked the London Transport records. Your call to the police was timed at 11:55pm. Why did it all take so long? We're talking about nearly a quarter of an hour here.'

Poor Jack. He looked thunderstruck. You'd have sworn Roderick had suddenly accused him of the murder. I was the only one in the courtroom who knew there hadn't been a murder of any kind. Everyone else – judge, jury and both counsel – was already clearly convinced, even at that early stage, of Jim Corcoran's guilt.

The rest of the trial was a farce, really.

'Well, Sir.' Jack glanced nervously at the judge. 'Like I said I was too stunned by what I'd seen on the screen to ring straight way and then I saw that man coming my way.'

Jack looked appealingly towards the judge.

'Perhaps I did wait five minutes or even a bit more after Corcoran had left before I rang the police. I was that scared. For all I knew, he might have come back in again and then … and then… The police will tell you that I was even afraid to go out on the station platform with them when they arrived.'

Roderick must have used the expression 'in the cause or furtherance of theft' a hundred times over the rest of the trial. Everyone in the courtroom quickly built up the same picture of what had happened on the night of 25th November 1959.

I even half-started to believe this fictitious version of events myself. Jim Corcoran had heard about 'all those fivers and oncers' in Steve Charles's wallet from Al in Parva-vale. So, he went back to see where Steve was in the station, then he'd tried to take the money by force as the two of them were the North Ruislip footbridge together, probably arguing. The argument soon became a fight. Neither Jack nor anyone else had actually witnessed any kind of confrontation between the two – but everyone in that courtroom was certain there'd been one.

In the struggle, they all thought, Steve fell to his death on the platform. Whether or not this was the result of a deliberate push was something the lawyers were prepared to be generous about, after a fashion.

Roderick said it was something for which absolute proof was not available. It was a matter between the members of the jury and their individual consciences, he said. I'm sure the judge should have said something here, but he held his peace. Anyway, Old Jack's evidence about Jim robbing the body was enough for the jury. It was more than enough.

This was the way it went on for ages more. Finally, the time came when one of the court blokes walked up to the judge with the black cap. In truth it wasn't a cap at all. It was no more than a square of black cloth. The judge couldn't put it on top of his silly wig and adjusted it so that one corner was pointed towards me – Jim Corcoran – quickly enough. Everyone could see this was the moment he'd been waiting for.

'… shall be taken to the place from whence you came, and from there be taken to a place of execution. You shall be hanged by the neck until the body be dead... dead... DEAD!'

He really hammered that little mallet thing in time with the last three words. He finished his stuff, with another, even worse, bit of theatrics.

'And may God have mercy upon your soul.'

Talbot, my defence counsel, looked at me briefly as if to say, *'you should have gone along with the insanity plea'*.

I thought that would be the last I'd see of him, but he and Barlow, the solicitor, did come to see me in the cells afterwards. Thus was a waste of time. It was supposed to be to outline any grounds for appeal against the sentence.

All they wanted to do was tell me there weren't any grounds if I wouldn't play along with the insanity business they were fixated on and get out of there. Well, I had enough time to think about it afterwards and it seemed there were plenty of grounds for appeal to me.

After they'd gone through the motions they marched out of the cell without a backward glance. No doubt they were anxious to be on their way back to normal legal work, hoping to find more promising material for the building of their careers.

*

The 'place of execution' chosen for me was HMP Wandsworth. It seemed this prison normally only hanged people from Surrey and Kent, but they were going to make an exception for me.

What I understand is that they were helping out HMP Pentonville. Wandsworth had dealt earlier in the month with a German who'd killed a policeman – oddly enough, at his trial he'd claimed he'd lost his memory – but the prison didn't have any other capital cases coming up. I wished they hadn't tried to be so helpful to busy Pentonville, where I'd normally have gone.

To be honest, I couldn't have too many complaints about my treatment in the prison. The food was quite OK and most of the warders were friendly enough. Frank and Will – I had to call them Mr Jenkins and Mr French in the hearing of their bosses – were the two I liked best.

Will French was a real character, always telling jokes. This was his first proper job after leaving school, so he'd have been younger than me. Frank Jenkins looked sideways at his colleague as if he disapproved, although the older man could never resist a chuckle at whatever Will said.

I was sure Will was in the pay of one of the Sunday papers. Thanks to the way Jack had given his evidence, the case was a minor sensation for the press boys.

They loved it, especially when it properly came out that I had indeed won a medal in Dunkirk. They wrote reams and reams about the way the war-hero-gone-wrong was supposed to have pushed 'Little Steve' off the bridge. In the end, I even became fed up with my surreptitious glances at Will's newspapers and stopped bothering.

Will was always trying to draw details of Jim's life from me, especially about his life since Dunkirk – it seemed Jim had fallen off the map after the war. I only wished I had some information to give him. As things were, he knew far more than I did about Jim's mixed life. Although I hope he didn't realise it, *I* was always trying to get information out of *him*.

*

One day, when we were alone together, after telling me one of his long, elaborate jokes, Will surprised me by suddenly putting his hand on my arm and asking a question.

'Tell me,' he said, 'what made you give up athletics so suddenly to join the army?'

This was a line he must have recently been fed by one of the blokes in the newspaper trade. Jim's aborted career on the track wasn't general knowledge at the time. But I could answer this one. I'd read Jim's scrapbook.

'Well, I could see the war coming. I wanted to join up and do my bit for my country.'

'Come off it.' Will laughed. 'A lot of people tell me they could see big trouble heading our way at the time, so they say now anyway, but nobody thought they could handle it on their own. They all waited for the call-up. There must have been more to it for you.'

'Well, there was some girl trouble. I wanted to get away her. I can't even remember her name now. It started with an M.'

I was making the bit about 'girl trouble' up. I had no idea what kind of relationship Jim had with this mystery woman. I might have been doing them both an injustice. Anyway, that was where I had to stop making up a story to please Will. I didn't know more than the initial of the forename of the girl. I wouldn't have known even this much, had I not chanced upon it in Cypress Close.

'I'm not surprised when you say it had something to do with a woman. What did you say her name was?'

Will was clearly fishing.

'I told you; I don't remember.'

I really knew nothing about this girl. Will looked as me as if he didn't believe what I was telling him. Then he smiled.

'Still, must have been a helluva thing, giving yourself to a life on the track and then finding yourself on Dunkirk beach a couple of years later, eh Jim?'

Dunkirk again. When I was a kid, I remembered my mother telling me my father had bought it in Dunkirk. Still, so did a great many other soldiers. I knew Den, my mate from the wallpaper factory, had been wounded during the Dunkirk evacuation. At least Jim Corcoran managed to get out with his life. He'd even been awarded a medal, although for some reason he hadn't impressed himself with whatever he'd done.

'I don't remember much about the war.'

I didn't remember *anything* about it. Steve Charles had half-memories of being carried down the steps of air raid shelters by his mother as a kid and the awful wail from the siren they used to call the Moaning Minnie. Jim could remember absolutely nothing.

'The story from wartime says your memory was wiped clean on that day. Must be true, then. Still, an officer from another unit remembered exactly what happened; that's how come they gave you the medal. You deserved a lot more than a piece of tin for what you did.'

I still said nothing. *I* wanted to see what Will was going to tell *me*.

'There were four of you together, mates you were, on the beach, is about all I've been able to find out. Two of the others were also strafed, but you insisted on dragging one of them – your best mate, so they say – to safety.

'As if that wasn't enough, you went back for the other one. You managed to drag him back to your unit, despite all the firing. How you managed to do that, no one knows. Pity the first poor devil was dead by the time you got back. You weren't so far off it yourself, so they tell me.'

'I don't remember a thing about it,' I said, flatly.

'No, of course you wouldn't,' said Will. 'You were in hospital for eight months. And then what did they do? They sent you back into the army, that's what they did. In 1944 you were back over in Europe, in Belgium this time. You didn't make the headlines then, but – hey – wasn't what you did in Dunkirk really something?'

It was what Jim Corcoran did, I mentally corrected Will. So far as I know, Steve Charles hadn't even been into a shelter in May 1940. I was around eighteen months old at that time.

'Then, after the war, there's nothing about you anywhere. They think you might have been somewhere in London for a few years. Then, just a year or two back, nobody has any real idea why, you went back to North Ruislip. That bit came out at the trial. It was where you lived before the war, but why did you do a thing like returning to North Ruislip, then?'

'Sorry, Mr French. I don't want to talk about the past anymore.'

At least it made a change from blaming my memory.

*

The thing I did most during those weeks in the prison was read. I was always asking them to get me something or other from the prison library. Funny thing, but since I'd left school, I'd read little but newspapers or, more often, comics. Books I found to be hard work. It was almost as if I was looking for something, although I didn't quite know what this could be. And then, on the first day of the new decade, I found it.

Goodness knows what the old book was doing in the prison library or why the title appealed to me as much as it did when I saw it on the tatty book lists they loaned to me. This title was *Ancient Egyptian Beliefs: A Focus on Death.*

Hardly thrilling stuff. I suppose it might have been because my mind was never far from the subject of my own end, a short time ahead, although I'd have thought this would have made me want to avoid the subject as far as I could.

When the book was eventually placed in my hands – Frank Jenkins told me the prison governor had doubts about its suitability as reading material for me in the condemned cell – I was at first reluctant to look inside its covers. The volume was battered and grimy. It had been published all of thirty-two years ago.

The writing was turgid. The wonder is that I made it as far as chapter five, about the soul. It seemed the Ancient Egyptians believed there were five parts to the soul: the *Ren*, the *Ba*, the *Ka*, the *Sheut*, and the *Ib*. Although the 'Ba', or roughly 'personality' seemed to be the most important in many ways, the 'Ka', roughly 'spirit' or 'vital spark' was the one that made me sit up and take notice.

I shivered at the idea that Steve Charles' – my – 'Ka', perhaps with help from his 'Ba', had somehow been so strong as to refuse to perish when Steve's body did. And, if it had happened to Steve Charles, could it happen again with Jim Corcoran's 'Ka' when his turn to make a publicised exit at the end of a rope came?

I was sure Steve was now the tenant of Jim's body, rather than Jim himself. Maybe he – I – could move house, so to speak, once again? An idea was beginning to form in my mind. Will French should have a long life before him. And he had a young wife he was always talking about…

*

'I'm a Roman Catholic! I want a proper priest; I don't want to see your prison chaplain!'

I have no idea what made me say this.

Frank Jenkins and Will French looked at me as if I'd said I wanted the Moon.

'But we didn't know you were religious in any way. It says clearly on your form *Religion: None.* What are we supposed to do at this late stage? Your execution is to be on Monday,' said Frank.

In a way, I was a Catholic. I hadn't thought of this when I had my solitary interview with the prison governor, Edward Darlington. One of my few shadowy memories of my mother was of her telling me my father used to be a regular attender at St Mary's before the war. I'd even been taken to the old church by her on a number of Sundays myself as a toddler, before she went off with the

American. This hardly qualified me as being one of the faithful, I know.

'I don't care what you do. Just get me a proper Priest.'

The result of my unaccustomed intransigence was an interview with Father Hubert Grey.

*

Father Grey was a gentle man in every sense. I didn't guess what a determined character lay beneath all that unhealthily pink flesh on our first acquaintance. He had little tufts of greying hair protruding beneath the peculiar little cowboy hat priests like to wear. A cowboy priest whose best days were now far behind him. That was my first impression of the churchman.

As soon as he came in the cell to see me, he took this hat from his head and held it before him, gazing into its crown as if it held all the answers anyone could ever want. It was a long time before he broke the silence. He cleared his throat and then said, almost inaudibly,

'Shall we pray together, my son?'

'I'm innocent, Father.'

Another, almost painful, silence followed.

'They've brought me in at a late stage. This prison is in an area outside my proper ministry. I'm really only here, you could say, because the prison governor and prison doctor are personal friends of mine.

'In these circumstances, there would be little point to the two of us discussing the matter of your guilt or otherwise. What you say to me will be bound by the seal of the confessional, let me assure you of this. When was the last time you made a confession?'

'I don't remember.'

In fact, I did. I'd never confessed in my whole life. Why should I? I wasn't really a Catholic and hadn't – either in my brief time as Jim Corcoran or anyone else – committed the crime for which Jim's body was soon going to be hanged. But why had I asked for this priest to be in my cell? I still wasn't sure why I had done this.

'My son, would you like to confess your sins before me now?'

'Couldn't we just talk for a while first?'

'Very well. What do you want to say?'

'Father, as Steve Charles I wasted my life, even though I committed no mortal sin, or no more than a very few small ones. Then I took over Jim Corcoran's life – I couldn't help that; it just happened – and now I'm wasting the last days of this life, too. Jim threw away the middle part of it all by himself, although I couldn't say why. It was something that happened in the war, I suppose what I am trying-'

Father Grey put his hands together. This gesture almost suggested that he was going to begin a prayer without me.

'May I stop you there, my son? It sounds to me as if you really do want to make a confession but don't know how to go about it. Could I suggest you spend the rest of today in private prayer and contemplation? You must ask for more guidance from the Lord than I, as a mere man, am able to give you.

'Tomorrow, I hadn't planned to visit you – I have my main Sunday services to conduct, you see. But I will certainly come to you straight afterwards if you need my help. Just send word via the prison authorities. I'll speak to the governor on my way home. Agreed? Meanwhile, I'll leave these notes for you. They may help.'

'Agreed.' What was I saying? I didn't know to what I was agreeing. Nor did I really know for what I was asking. 'But you will be here on Monday morning, even if I do nothing?'

Yes, Monday was the day I was to be hanged. Saying it that way made it seem so much closer.

'Naturally, I will, my son. Of course I will.'

Needless for me to say, I didn't send word to Father Grey later that day, nor on Sunday. The notes he gave me were just homilies with silly cartoons. They didn't help in the least. But I did pray, or at least I tried to – to contemplate, if that is the right word.

I even thought for a moment of confessing on Jim's behalf – of confessing to the murder I was absolutely sure he didn't commit. I knew this would be as wrong as anything could be. It would be wrong for me – spiritually immoral, if you like, as well as useless. It would be so much worse for Jim.

For the rest of that weekend, I almost went mad. It was only Will French's jokes that saved me from tipping over the edge on Sunday evening.

*

On Sunday morning I was given what I thought was a special treat. At first my belief was that it was strictly unofficial and Darlington, the prison governor couldn't have been such a bad bloke after all.

Will and Frank weren't on duty in the morning – anyway, I'd have more need for their steadying presence in the evening and most especially on the next morning, when I was due to be topped – so Butter and his morose partner Yates took me on a long walk.

Butter was my least favourite of the warders. At least on my last full morning he had the decency to be silent. As we reached the furthest exercise yard I was actually thinking *'This is good of them.'*

The weather was mild and pleasant for January; the sun was even shining wanly. For a moment it was almost possible to forget where I was and what awaited me at nine o'clock the next day. Then, with cold horror, I abruptly realised exactly why they'd brought me all the way out here.

I started to remember all the dark stories about the way they took the condemned man out of his cell so that the hangman could go through his warm-up routine, starting with whatever it was he did first in the special room behind the condemned cell.

On the way out they'd weighed me and measured my height. *Just routine*, Butter and Yates had assured me breezily. I realised that I was here purely to allow the hangman and his assistant to be free to dangle a bag of sand of the same weight as me in what would soon be my place. The rope, so I'd heard, would be left attached to the sandbag overnight to remove any stretch.

If you'll pardon the expression, they didn't hang about in those days. The trial was over well before Christmas, so I didn't find myself as HMP Wandsworth's special guest for very long.

There was a rule that four Sundays had to pass before a death sentence could be put into effect. Goodness knows why this was. It was some ancient tradition, I suppose. They were very fond of their old rules in the death business. The third Monday in January – 18th January 1960, if you want the exact date – was my appointed day.

On the evening before, Frank and Will ended their shift almost in high spirits. They were trying to cheer me up, I suppose. Still, I was grateful to do my best to go along with the mood.

Even Frank joined in with Will's outrageous jokes about the 'little ghouls from the schools'. You can guess the sort of thing: they should set a homework essay on the subject; it should be organised as a proper outing for the little bleeders; concern as to whether their mothers had packed sandwiches for them. There was a lot more – well, 'gallows humour' I suppose you'd have to call it, flying around on that Sunday evening.

Many of the schoolchildren in Wandsworth would be late for school on an execution day because, shortly before nine o'clock on those days, they'd love to congregate in large numbers as close as they could to the prison gates. Why?

*

Early on the Monday morning – they'd especially arranged to do this shift to support me, even after being on duty on the Sunday afternoon shift – none of the three of us could even begin to lift our spirits. Poor Frank Jenkins looked like he was on the verge of tears and Will French was silent for the first time during the weeks I'd known him.

I'd been given back my own – Jim's own – clothes to wear. They were returned fresh from the prison laundry, looking almost presentable. I knew exactly what it meant when they were taken from the white bag. I wasn't going to be wearing them for long.

Father Grey had arrived a full half hour ago. At first, he'd tried to make some conversation, but I really didn't want to know. Then he tried once again to make me confess. Confess? To what did anyone have to confess? Now he sat silent in the corner, failure written all over his fat face. He'd failed all right, even though his heart was in the right place – in a manner of speaking it was, at least.

Suddenly, I heard the tiniest sound from behind the wardrobe-thing next to the back wall of my cell. After that everything happened so quickly. Frank and Will stepped forward and, in one easy movement, slid the lightweight wardrobe aside to reveal what we all knew was there, a metal door. This they pushed open to reveal a very ordinary looking man in a three-piece suit.

There were some others, all male, already waiting in the execution chamber, but I scarcely had time to take this in. This was the first time I'd seen the public hangman, in life or even in a photograph, but I knew the moment I saw him that he was the man who was going to take my life.

'*How can you do a job like this*?' I thought.

Almost before I realised what was happening, he'd stepped forward smartly and stood behind me. Then he bound my wrists with a strap. My binding felt as though it was made from hard, new leather. After this, he turned back to return from whence he'd come, the gallows chamber.

Frank and Will grabbed me, one on each side, and hurried me after the hangman. They marched me towards the trapdoor, which helpfully had a large 'T' chalked onto it.

There were boards on either side of the trapdoor. My warders hustled me forward onto these. Frank and Will were both stony-faced. Then the hangman pulled a white hood over my head and smartly put the noose over it – this had been suspended before me – and quickly tied it up with a thread.

The thread couldn't have been tied very well. Some of it found its way under the hood and briefly tickled my chin, I remember. The petty things you recall from a time like that, eh? At the same time, one of the others in the chamber – I wasn't sure which, the assistant hangman, I suppose – had bent down to strap my ankles.

Seconds after he'd finished this I heard a 'clunk'. I knew this sound to be the hangman operating the lever. Immediately, I knew a dropping sensation and felt the rope biting painfully into my neck as it was wrenched sideways.

[3] Hubert

Something was wrong. My idea had been to take over the body of Will French by making a pure effort of will. It wasn't to be as easy as this. I'd been concentrating hard on my target for the last ten minutes. But there he was, standing close to me, his image dancing crazily in my blurred vision, looking at me with concern.

As my eyes started to come into a more normal focus, I could see that, standing on the opposite side of the open trapdoor, was an equally worried-looking Frank Jenkins. Below the trapdoor, the hooded corpse of Jim Corcoran slowly twisted right and left at the end of the hangman's rope.

There were no fewer than seven other men in the chamber. I knew Will and Frank of course. The Governor, Edward Darlington, and the Public Hangman were, to start with, the only others I recognised. From what I'd been told earlier I worked out the other three must be Sir Henry Mountjoy, the Lord Lieutenant of the County, the prison doctor, and the hangman's assistant, but at that point I wasn't sure which might be which.

I didn't wonder for long, because a searing pain, starting in my left arm, then quickly spreading into the depths of my chest, sharply brought every bit of my attention back to myself.

'Are you all right, Father?' said Will, stepping forward. His expression was still an anxious one.

Father! How could such a thing be? I should be Will himself!

'He should be fine in a moment – I'm afraid some of us have seen this before – although I do think he should have a good hour's rest in my office before he leaves the prison. I won't take long about doing the final examination of the deceased and then I'll walk the Father back, nice and steadily.' said Dr Young.

Dr Young? How did I now know the prison doctor's name?

Sir Henry Mountjoy and Mr Darlington nodded their agreement. Suddenly, I found I even knew what the public hangman and his assistant were called: Harry Allen and Roy Rickard. What was going on?

Dr Young had to give me physical support as we walked back to his office. By that time, my chest pains were beginning to subside, although my legs were aching abominably. My eyesight was starting to come back into something like a more normal sort of focus, but my whole frame was incredibly weak, and my mind was in a swirl.

'That old ticker giving you trouble again, Hubert?' Young said. as soon as he'd helped me sit in his easy chair. 'If you don't mind my saying so, or even if you do, I really think it's time for you to call it a day on this sort of duty. All the extracurricular work you do, especially. This prison is across the river from your own parish, after all.'

'If a man needs my help, whether inside or outside my parish, I have no choice but to come to him. In this case, Edward Darlington couldn't go through normal channels at such a late stage. Edward has been a friend of mine since he was assistant governor in Pentonville. So, I had to be the one to come to talk to his condemned prisoner.'

These were the words I spoke, but not those I thought. The sentence seemed to form itself on my lips of its own accord.

We chatted inconsequentially for another thirty minutes. Father Hubert Grey now, crazily, me, and Dr Andy Young – I knew everyone's first names into the bargain by this time – clearly knew each other well.

The doctor even gave me a more thorough examination with the aid of the bigger stethoscope he kept in his office. Then he placed a small glass of brandy in my hand. This was clearly intended quite as much for social purposes as for any medical reason. He joined me in having one for himself. Then, again entirely unexpected by me, I found myself rising to my feet.

'I really have to get back,' I said.

In truth I'd been sitting there, hoping he'd offer me another, larger, brandy. Now the pain had eased, it was almost pleasant to find myself relaxed in a comfortable chair in the doctor's office, with the winter sunshine streaming in through the window. This was especially true after the morning I'd had, but a strong will – it could only that of Hubert Grey – was somehow driving me on.

'Oh no you don't, Hubert. You sit there. I'll go and fetch your driver. He can walk you back to the car at a good, slow pace'.

I remained sitting in the armchair, trying to work out what had happened. It was true that I had been thinking about how unfair it might be for me to be taking over Will French's body as I'd planned. He was a young man whose whole life was before him. But I thought I'd had it all worked out. Will's life would continue with a new man behind the steering wheel, in a manner of speaking. It wasn't to be as simple as this.

Will had made a point of telling me he had a young, pretty wife. Making her acquaintance had been uppermost in my mind, I have to admit. Steve Charles had been a cock virgin, in the unkind expression Al from Parva-vale had loved to use as a frequent part of his not-so-gentle teasing.

There was no doubt that Father Hubert Grey was an interesting, if worrying, man. He was at least sixty years old and was in decidedly poor health. I'd thought at first when I met him in the condemned cell that he was no more than out of shape; now I'd had closer experience than I wanted of exactly how unwell he was. Even Sir Henry Mountjoy, the Lord Lieutenant of the County, who was probably at least five years the priest's senior, would have been a better bet for a new body.

Then the office door opened and in walked Andy Young with Ken Barker, my driver. I was hardly surprised to find I knew the driver's full name.

'A steady walk back to the car now, Ken, don't forget,' said Andy. 'Take it easy. Father Grey has had another of his turns.'

'Don't worry, Doctor,' said the young man. 'We're becoming used to this routine, I'm afraid. Slow and stately all the way home it'll be for us. That's the way I'll drive the car, too. Ready, Father?'

I nodded, not wanting to speak. I didn't know whose words would issue from my lips.

'I'll call in to see you at home to see how you're progressing next week, Hubert,' said Dr Young. 'Try to take it easy between now and then, won't you?'

You could see by their expressions that they knew Father Grey wouldn't have the slightest intention of 'taking it easy'. The doctor especially seemed to know this would be the case.

'Ask your own doctor to come out to give you a more thorough going over as soon as he can, too,' said Andy Young. 'I know I'm wasting my breath in saying these things but promise me you'll at least think about it for once, please.'

He smiled.

'Well, at any rate, now I'll be going home myself to relax for a few hours on this bright Monday morning. This is far and away the worst part of the job. The moment when I have to bend down and listen to the prisoner's heart fluttering to a stop really gets to me. Yes, a few hours on my reclining chair. That's the thing for me now. A feet up job is what I need now.'

Poor Jim. A brief time ago he'd been hanging, feet down, in a chamber at the back of the condemned cell. He hadn't had much of a life. The bit of it I'd shared with him must have been the worst part of it, although whatever he went through at Dunkirk must have been bad to have changed his life so completely.

Or would it even be accurate for me to think I'd shared it with him? He didn't seem to have contributed to our joint existence beyond a few vague feelings filtering through to Steve Charles's awareness. Hubert Grey was clearly going to be a different prospect.

Anyway, there could no denying this was my third life, or at least this would be the third body I'd inhabited in not much more than a month. This third existence hadn't started very promisingly, trapped in the body of a sick old man as I found myself to be. When I'd taken over Jim's life, I'd gained more than twenty years in an instant. Now I'd gained at least another twenty years and dangerously fragile health to boot.

*

Ken, my driver, proved to be an engaging young man. He kept up a stream of constant chatter on our journey home. I was content to remain silent as far as I could. Although by some mysterious means I seemed to know some detail of the clergyman's life, this knowledge was patchy in the extreme.

I wanted to know where we were going – where exactly was this 'home' Ken and Andy had been talking about? This was one of the many pieces of information I was missing. I was trying to think of an oblique way of getting this information out of Ken when, while we were crossing Putney Bridge, he casually mentioned that we were on our way to Ealing.

Ealing? I knew Ealing. It wasn't too far from the wallpaper factory in Parva-vale where I – Steve Charles I suppose I should say – had worked. So much had happened in recent weeks that it was hard to believe it was only last November I was a factory worker in Parva-vale. This wasn't even two full months ago.

'Don't go straight home, Ken,' I said, surprising myself with my words. 'I want to take a little diversion first. You know where I want to go. To the place on the riverside. After all, this is where I'd have been going today if I hadn't been suddenly called to Wandsworth prison.'

Even if Ken Barker *did* know of the place Hubert Grey was thinking of I, as Steve Charles, certainly didn't. It was disconcerting, to say the least, to have two competing wills living in the same body.

'But Father,' my driver responded. 'Dr Young will be so angry if I didn't take you straight home. Mrs Broadbent would tell me off, too, once she hears you've had another turn.'

'Who pays your wages, young man? Dr Young, Mrs Broadbent or me?'

'I'm sorry Father.'

Ken lapsed into silence. I felt regret at my harsh reprimand. I had no idea who Mrs Broadbent might be. Another blank patch in this peculiar memory I now possessed.

'Don't worry, Ken. I know you had my interests at heart. We're probably a bit too late, anyway. We'll go straight back to Ealing now.'

'Thank you, Father.'

'How long have you been my driver, now?'

'Nearly three years now, Sir.'

'Then it's high time I raised your pay, wouldn't you say?'

'But you gave me more money less than six months ago. I'm paid seven pounds now. That's very generous for a job like this.'

Seven pounds? That was nearly a pound more than Steve Charles had been paid in the wallpaper factory. The two young men were around the same age, with Ken Barker being perhaps a year or two older. And he was the one who'd landed on his feet.

Steve hadn't. I shuddered when I realised the literal meaning of this thought. Steve Charles had landed on his head, not his feet, when he fell down the footbridge in North Ruislip station.

'Well, as from next week, I'm going to give you an extra ten shillings a week, anyway. You can be sure of it. Tell me, do you like your job, Ken?'

It was Hubert Grey who'd asked this question but I, as Steve Charles, was also interested to hear what Ken would answer.

'Thank you so much. I'm going to give it all to my mother. She has so little. This is the best job in the world, Father.'

To go by the enthusiastic tone of his voice, he meant exactly what he'd said, too.

'Coming to work as your driver was the finest thing that ever could have happened to me.'

I wondered what Ken's life had once been. Hoping Father Hubert didn't already know this, I ventured a question.

'Remind me, what did you do before this driving job, Ken?'

'It's something I remember all too well, myself. I'd been a member of your congregation for years. You'd heard I knew how to drive. I'd learned to drive the van at the factory so they could have a spare driver. My chance for anything better than the daily drudge never came up. It looked like a life on the shop floor for me. It flabbergasted me when, one day after church, you asked me if I'd like to come and work for you. I jumped at the chance to escape from that fire extinguisher factory in Parva-vale.'

Parva-vale? Ken and Steve seemed to have a lot in common.

'Were your parents pleased when you changed your job?'

'My mother was, even if, when you moved to your new church, it meant me moving from our house in Parva-vale to your own new one in Ealing.' Ken's smooth face took on a serious expression.

'I thought you'd remember, Sir. I never knew my father.' Ken looked at me sideways. I should be more careful with my questions. 'He died in Dunkirk when I was still a baby. I hope you don't mind me repeating this, but you're the nearest thing I've had to a father, as I was telling you only the other day.'

Dunkirk? The word acted like a cold spear in my gut. When I heard Ken saying it, I couldn't think of what else to ask him. Anyway, I didn't have the chance to say more, because he was soon swinging the car right into a wide, tree-lined road. This led to another, if anything broader, avenue. I noticed the name on an ancient road sign: Hanover Street.

This wasn't a part of Ealing I knew. It was far plusher than any area I'd ever visited. Ken crunched the cars' wheels into a gravelly drive on the left-hand side of the avenue, parked efficiently, and applied the handbrake.

Clearly, Father Grey must have had some private money. He'd never have been able to employ a chauffeur on a church living – although they used the more straightforward word 'salary' in the Catholic Church, didn't they?

How on Earth did I know this? Another scrap of information from the priest's inconsistent memory.

'Everything all right, Father?' Ken asked, as he came around to my side of the car. He seemed to be surprised to find I'd already opened the car door and was getting out unaided.

'Of course. I'm perfectly fine,' I said. But I was far from being perfectly fine. My legs were shaking from making the mere effort of getting out of the car. I was sweating after the effort of standing for only a few seconds.

'Please don't overexert yourself, Father.'

I favoured Ken with what I hope looked more like a smile than a scowl.

'Mrs Broadbent will be– ah, here she is now,' he said.

The front door of the house opened, and a short, rotund woman stepped out. She was clearly the housekeeper. So, Father Grey could afford to employ someone to keep house for him as well as to equip his chauffeur with an expensive car.

'I hope things went well for the two of you gentlemen? I do worry when the Father goes on one of what he calls his special missions, even though he'll never tell me what is involved in them.'

'Not really,' said Ken, speaking before I had the chance to say anything. 'The Father had another one of his turns. It was at the very moment of the execution, so Dr Young informed me.'

At this, Mrs Broadbent's happy expression changed to one of concern. Showing a surprising turn of speed, she rushed over to where I was standing next to the car and seized my elbow.

'An execution? Oh, Father Grey! You remember what happened the last time you went to one of those,' she said, grasping my arm tightly. 'Ken, help me get the Father to his room. He needs to lie down for an hour or two.'

'Please don't make a fuss, Mrs Broadbent.'

Again, I heard myself saying the opposite of what I was thinking. A quiet rest was exactly what I thought this sick old body could do with. This was my own thinking. But, once more, something prevented me from giving voice to my thought.

'Well, at least you must have a quiet sit-down in your favourite leather armchair in the study for a while,' she said. She eased her grip on my arm as she said this, walking me slowly towards the front door. 'I'll bring you your lunch in on a tray in an hour. Absolutely no reading or writing for you this morning. Promise me you'll just sit quietly for once.'

As we stepped inside the front door, a thought worried me. I had no clue as to where this study might be. Mrs Broadbent released my arm and looked up at me, smiling nervously in the hallway. I simply stood there. What else could I do?

'Would you like me to walk you to your study?' She looked anxiously up towards my face. 'Are you quite sure you're well enough to go on your own?''

'Mrs Broadbent, I'm perfectly fine.'

This I was not. Father Grey wasn't feeling anything like fine and Steve didn't have a clue as to where he should be going.

'Ken, will take you and get you settled in your chair, won't you Ken? You always did have a way with the Father, Ken. He'll listen to you when he takes no mind of me.'

Thank goodness for that. Ken linked his arm easily with mine and gently guided me towards the second door on the right. I noticed the refined gentility of the hall's furnishings and the tasteful burnishing of the staircase we passed on the left. Father Grey clearly lived well.

The study I found to be small but cosy. The room was dominated by a huge, highly polished desk and a number of full bookshelves. These, and an inviting swivel chair, took up a large part of the available space. The shelves were crammed with books of every description. Most of the bindings were modest but my eyes alighted on two broad shelves full of books with luxurious covers.

'Your favourite books, eh father? I can see why. I love this room myself. I was so glad when Mrs Broadbent wanted me to come in here today. It's not often I get the chance to see it. Well, I must get you settled in, as she says.'

The young man led me over to the soft leather chair and helped me to sit down. Then he covered my knees with a thick blanket.

'Thank you, Ken.'

'No books or writing for you today, I'm sorry. Mrs Broadbent has spoken wisely. Please, please, just take it easy. Well, I must be off and let you get your rest before she brings your lunch in.'

'One moment, Ken. You'd started to tell me about your early life on the way home this morning. Tell me some more, please.'

Ken looked at me doubtfully.

'There's not much to tell, Sir. You know most of the story already.'

'Nevertheless…' Would Father Grey have used a word like this? The priest's consciousness seemed to be becoming dormant at this moment. Was it really me, Steve Charles, who wanted to know more about Ken? I was certainly interested to hear what he was going to say.

'My parents married in 1937. Just after they found out I was on the way, it was. My father's job in the army – he'd not long become a regular soldier – was getting very active with all the training manoeuvres and so on at the time. They would have let him come home to see his baby son, but he thought he shouldn't take leave at a time when so much was happening.

'As everyone knows, war did break out. Not long afterwards, my father went to France. He died on the beach in Dunkirk, so I never did see him, and he never saw me. That's all I can tell you. I know my father only through photographs and from my mother's stories.'

'Some story, Ken. Life must have been hard for you and your mother.'

'It was hard.' Ken looked down. 'But you and St Mary's in North Ruislip helped my mother a lot. You'd already been the priest for quite a few years then, of you remember.

'This was why we both continued to travel to North Ruislip for church after we had to move to Parva-vale because of my work. My mother was overjoyed when you were able to give me this job, even though by then you'd moved on to the bigger St Mary's in Ealing. Church was important to her.'

'Ken!' A sudden thought came to me. 'Did you ever know a boy by the name of Stephen Charles?'

The young man looked surprised at my question.

'Well, we were both from Parva-vale, although I couldn't say I knew him, exactly.'

He looked at me closely, with concern on his features.

'But you knew who he was!'

'Well, now I know who he was. Most of us do, Father.'

Ken was looking very doubtful about continuing. But he did.

'He – a young man rather than a boy – was the victim in that murder case. You went to see the murderer in Wandsworth Prison a few times as part of your work, Sir. He, Jim Corcoran by name, was hanged only this morning. I was waiting outside. You were there, in the death-cell itself. You remember, don't you Father? You are OK now, aren't you?'

He looked at me quizzically. Did he think Father Grey's mind as well as his body was fragile? I really should be more careful with my questions. But something drove me on.

'When you lived in Parva-vale, did you know a man called Al or Alan Milgram? Was he a relative of yours? Perhaps on your father's side?' I was clutching at straws.

Ken's expression now became one of real puzzlement and concern.

'No, I've never known anyone by that name. My mother didn't keep in touch with my father's friends. And we had few relatives on my father's side. He, Tommy Barker, was an only child, I believe. At least, my mother never spoke of anyone except for my grandparents who lived on the other side of London. I never saw them. They didn't want to know us after my father went. That's the way my mother put it.'

'Did…?' I wasn't sure what I was trying to find out.

'I'm sorry, Father,' Ken said. 'I really do think you should rest now. Otherwise, Mrs Broadbent will be in here telling me off for tiring you out. We can continue this conversation another time.'

I slumped back in the chair. Perhaps Father Grey would let me rest now. We both needed it.

*

For four days my world became the tiny one whose boundaries were marked out by my study, my bedroom, the upstairs bathroom, and the staircase that connected them. It was always Mrs Broadbent who helped me on the stairs.

Ken kept out of the way. I knew I'd made far too much of the fact that he'd lived at one time in both Parva-vale and North Ruislip. There were also a few parallels between his early life and my own – Steve Charles' own, that is. Barker is hardly the rarest of surnames. And, sadly, a great many soldiers hadn't made it off the beach in Dunkirk.

Mrs Broadbent seemed content to be nursing an invalid, bringing each one of my meals in on a tray and otherwise happily fussing around. She wouldn't have been happy if she knew I'd made a practice of limping over to examine the bookshelves, whenever she wasn't around.

He had an impressive collection of books, Father Grey. By no means were they all volumes on theology, either. Those I've read from cover to cover since that time include *The Planet Jupiter* by Bertrand M Peek, only published two years before I found a copy on Father Grey's shelves, Sir James Jeans's *The Universe Around Us* and HJR Murray's *A History of Chess*. Back then, it was the titles and splendid bindings I was taken by. I didn't do much real reading.

But I was a different person in those days. In more ways than one was I a different person.

Father Grey's strong will seemed to be in a period of quietude during this rest period, too. It was a kind of holiday for me, although I couldn't help thinking I was on something of a convalescent holiday, with me trying to take care of the body of a sick man. Still, this time wasn't bad as long as it lasted. But on the fifth day I felt the impatient priest stirring within me.

*

'Are you sure you're ready to go out today, Father?'

'Ken, you nag me quite as much as Mrs Broadbent. Mondays and Fridays are the best days for me to find Victor in that particular spot. I need to go today if I want to talk to him. That's all there is to it.'

What particular spot? These words may have come from Steve Charles's new lips, but most definitely he didn't want to go. Father Grey's will may have been eager to be off on some mysterious chase – mysterious to me, that is – but I dearly wanted to stay in the nice, warm study and be surrounded by the splendour of those book covers.

*

Mrs Broadbent hovered on the doorstep, looking uncomfortable.

'I wish you'd at least tell me where you two are going, Father. Ken knows, but you've instructed him not to say a word to me,' she said.

The fact that the chauffeur knew something she didn't clearly irritated her.

'Don't worry, Mrs Broadbent,' was all I could say. The housekeeper looked so miserable

I wished I could answer her. But I couldn't say a word that would mean anything. I didn't even know where we were going myself.

'Ken, you make sure you look after him. Do you hear me?'

'I'll do my best, Mrs Broadbent.'

The housekeeper went inside the house, shaking her head sorrowfully as she closed the front door behind her.

In the car, Ken turned to me.

'At least let me come right down to the river with you this time.'

'You can't do that, Ken,' I heard myself saying. 'Last week I was at last making some progress with Victor. Do you want me to throw it all away, just when I'm starting to make some headway? No more of this, now.'

Victor? Who on Earth was this person called Victor? I had no idea.

As I was pondering this I caught sight in the passenger-side mirror of a man walking up the drive towards Ken and myself. I recognised him. It was, unbelievably, Al – Alan Milgram from the wallpaper factory in Parva-vale. What was he doing here?

'Father,' Al said to me through my open window as soon as he reached us, 'I need a word with you. It is so important to me.'

'I'm sorry, my son. I'm off on a crucial mission of salvation. Come and see me after Mass on Sunday.'

Al looked uncomfortable. He shifted from foot to foot.

'But I'm not a Catholic.'

'Not a Catholic? Then you must see your own minister.'

'I haven't got a minister. I don't go to any church.'

I partially opened the car door with difficulty.

'Then I really don't see why you think I could help you,' I said. 'There are people, non-religious people, to whom you could speak in confidence. I've got some names and addresses in a notebook I keep in my study. Ken, would you mind fetching…'

Al was red faced and looked almost tearful. I'd never seen him like this.

'No!' He looked contrite at the loud volume of his voice as he spoke. 'I'm sorry, Father. I didn't mean to raise my voice. This is something only you can help me with. I need to talk to you about Jim Corcoran.'

'Corcoran? The man who was hanged in Wandsworth Prison on Monday?' Father Grey was surprised. Both of us who shared this body were surprised.

'That's the one. I found out you saw him in his last hours. I need to confess – I did him wrong during the war and now I've done it again.'

He certainly didn't do Jim Corcoran a lot of good with his testimony at the murder trial, I thought. But it was Father Grey who held his own hand up.

'You can't confess to me. I'm sorry. What is your name? I could recommend someone-'

Al interrupted.

'My name is Alan Milgram. Most people call me Al. I'd join your church, do anything. Any penance, I mean. That's what you call them, isn't it?'

The priest sighed deeply. Both of us felt that sigh.

'Very well. I can see you need to talk.'

It was Father Grey who said this. I, Steve Charles, dearly wished Al would shut up and go away.

'But I really should be somewhere else now and this sounds like it may be a long story. You come back to my house at ten o'clock tomorrow and we'll talk. Only talk, mind. I make no promises.'

'But...' Al's shoulders slumped. 'Yes, I understand. Thank you, Father.'

With that, Al turned on his heel and trudged down the drive. I'd never seen before anyone with such a look of abject misery on his face. And this was Al, my oppressor – Steve's oppressor – from the wallpaper factory.

'Best wind that window up now, Father,' said Ken, turning the ignition key. 'We don't want to let too much cold January air in with us.'

*

'Well, what was all that about?' said Ken as he turned out of Hanover Street. 'I'm sorry Father. I know it's not my place to...'

'Don't worry Ken. I wish I knew myself. It looks as if I'm going to find out tomorrow.'

Did I even want to find out?

Ken lapsed into silence as we drove away. This suited me. The strangest thoughts and feelings were going on inside my head.

As each mile of our journey went by, I felt the consciousness of Father Grey was definitely receding and that of Steve Charles was coming once again to the fore. Passing down Chiswick High Street, over Kew Bridge and through Lower Richmond was a very strange experience: a kind of war had been going on inside of me but at last it felt as if I – Steve – was starting to win it. By the time we were travelling along Putney Bridge Road, I felt in complete control of myself once again.

The car cruised along Wandsworth Bridge Road and turned left towards the river into a part of London with which I was entirely unfamiliar. We turned left into an exceptionally slummy street with houses dating back at least to the eighteenth-century. The buildings were in various states of disrepair. The street seemed to be populated only by a few waif-like children. Ken pulled up the car next to the last house.

'Where are we?'

'Jews' Row, of course. Where you've been going for all these weeks. I'll bring the car back in exactly one hour as usual, that's at twenty to twelve. You know I can't park here. The children will throw stones at the car. Or worse. One hour, now. Please don't be late, Father.'

I was perplexed. Why did Father Grey want to come here? It was nowhere near his parish in a comparatively genteel part of Ealing. It was on the other side of the Thames, for a start. I suppose it must be like his work in Wandsworth Prison. That wasn't strictly official. This was surely much less so.

'But what am I here to do?'

Ken looked at me, a worried look on his face.

'You're here to meet Victor, as you've been doing for the last two months. Who he may be and what the two of you talk about I have no idea. Are you quite sure everything is well with you, Father?'

No, everything was far from well. I had no idea where I was to meet Victor, nor even who he was. But, again, I didn't want Ken to think Father Grey was becoming weak in the head as well as in the body.

I had the odd feeling, or perhaps it was no more than a hope, that I wasn't going to be plagued by the priest's intransigent personality and stubborn will again, at least for a while. More than anything else, I dearly wanted to enjoy his comfortable lifestyle in Ealing for as long as I could. I decided to try to bluff things out.

'Where did I arrange to meet Victor this time?'

'I don't know. You've never taken me.' Ken looked very doubtful. 'You always go somewhere around that corner, leading to the downstream walkway. Wouldn't you rather I drove you straight back to Ealing?'

'Only teasing, Ken. See you in an hour.'

It was a struggle to scramble up from the car seat with some degree of grace. My heavy breathing and pins and needles in my left arm and chest reminded me, as if I needed reminding, of just how unwell Father Grey was. I closed the car door with a gentle click. Ken still looked worried, but I waved at him as I walked away and tried to smile. With reluctant slowness, he pulled off. Now I was on my own.

*

In 1960 the Thames at this point was disgracefully filthy. The sides of the river were defined uncertainly by huge mud banks as I followed the river downstream, along Battersea Reach. Was I even going the right way? I had seen no one.

Then, I did see a lone person, not too far ahead. His figure was almost faded into the sombre background.

He was a man in his early middle years, thoroughly dirty and unkempt. He was sitting on a metal drum that at one time might have been blue in colour. The collar of his grubby overcoat was turned up against the cold of the January morning. As I approached, he turned his features, etched with an angry scowl, towards me. He said nothing until I was almost upon him.

'Father. You're late today.'

'Victor?'

'Who did you expect to find here? The Queen?'

I tried to laugh, although I found the man's manner brusque, even offensive.

'We're just here for the usual chat, Victor.'

Would Father Grey have said this?

'As long as you don't want to get me to praying again, like last week. You didn't come at all on Monday.'

'No, I'm afraid I was unwell.' With a start I remembered that Jim Corcoran had been hanged only five days ago, early on Monday morning. For the rest of those five days. I had been trapped within the ailing body of an unbelievably saintly priest – or should I say, I'd been sharing it with him. It seemed to me I'd too often had the smaller share, into the bargain.

'Well, I'll answer your questions, just as long as you don't try to make them too personal. But no praying, eh? Perhaps you'd be able to spare me a few bob more this time. Those people you were so keen for me to go and see wouldn't play ball one little bit. Showed me the bloody door, they did.'

'Oh?' I wondered what Victor, at Father Grey's prompting, had been up to. I decided to try to find out more. 'Why was that?'

Victor looked at me slyly.

'All the nosey questions they wanted to ask,' he said. 'And all those stupid forms. A man's got a right to some privacy, even when he's down on his luck.'

What could I say? I tried to give an inconsequential answer,

'Perhaps you should have played along with them.'

He looked at me as if I was some species of idiot.

'I gave them my proper name, too, like you said. They went all funny when I didn't have a birth certificate to show I really was Victor Smith. Nothing wrong with a name like that.'

'Smith? Your family name is Smith?' My mind started to race. 'Please tell me Victor, were you in the army? Did you go to France? Dunkirk, perhaps?'

'You know my name is Smith and that I served King and Country in the bleedin' army. I've told you all that stuff before.'

He regarded me suspiciously.

'I'm sorry, Victor. It's just that you might be related to someone I know.' His look remained doubtful. 'There could be some money in it for you.'

Could there? I knew there were some banknotes in Father Grey's wallet.

'Just answer my questions if you wouldn't mind. Were you in Dunkirk? The big evacuation? And – this could be important – did you or your family ever live in Parva-vale or North Ruislip?'

The man, this Victor, squinted at me. Clearly, he was wondering at my motives for asking these questions.

'You're way off target there, Chum.' He laughed shortly. 'No, I wasn't conscripted until

1941 so none of that Dunkirk malarkey for me. I went to France, yes, but that wasn't until the end of 1944.

'And before the war I was living in the Midlands. My family were from West Bromwich if you must know. I've never even heard of them places you're on about. Now, you said something about money…?'

West Bromwich! I should have noticed that accent before. Smith was a common name, after all. This might not be his real name, anyway. I was guessing wildly again.

'I think…' I didn't find out what Hubert Grey thought. Instead, I felt a vice-like grip tightening in my chest. The pain was far worse than anything I'd felt on Monday in the prison, only a mile from here.

Victor's face became angrier, and his lips were parted. He was clearly trying to tell me something, although I couldn't hear a word he was saying, or shouting.

Dully, and through increasingly blurring vision, I watched his mouth opening and closing. Then his head seemed to swing in an arc in front of me. The next thing I knew, the back of my skull was bouncing off the concrete walkway.

Then Victor's features loomed down towards mine. He still seemed to be shouting at me – I could even discern the small showers of spittle around his fast-moving lips – but I could hear not a word.

Then I felt his hand slipping into the inside pocket of the jacket underneath my winter coat. I felt a few hasty fumbles as its fingers grasped my calfskin wallet. I felt nothing more.

[4] Victor

There was an expensive-looking, soft leather wallet in my hand and a dead man lying, glassy-eyed, at my feet. There was no blood or bruising I could see, but I was quite sure he was dead. Had I murdered him for this wallet? It looked as though there could be no other explanation.

Somehow, I knew whose corpse this was: Father Grey of St Mary's in Ealing. But who was I? And what was either of us doing here, on the banks of a particularly dirty stretch of what looked to be the River Thames?

I was filled with panic at the thought of the crime only I could have committed. There was no one else in sight. Clearly, I should get away from here as soon as I could. I looked about me, trying to understand exactly where 'here' could be and recognised practically nothing. It was a grimy place in London close to the river, although exactly where on the Thames it might be I could not pinpoint.

At that moment, a yellow plastic ball rolled slowly around the side of the broken wall near to me and spiralled gently to a stop just yards from where I stood. Its owner would surely be following.

'Keithy!' came a plaintive cry from somewhere on the other side of the wall. The owner of the voice sounded like a little girl of perhaps seven or eight. 'You shouldn't keep hitting the ball towards the river. My mum doesn't like me going so close to the water. She keeps saying that Mole Gardner was drowned in this spot only last year.'

'Didn't mean to do it did I, Linda?' This slightly older sounding voice must have been Keith's in response.

'Well, I'm not going for it again this time. I'm going home to tell my mother.'

Some moments of silence passed.

'If you get the ball, Linda, you can go in and have a proper turn to bat. I promise I won't knock it over the wall next time I'm in, either.'

'Really promise? Cross your heart and hope to die promise?'

'Yeah, all right.'

'Promise properly or I won't go.'

'Oh, all right then. Cross my heart and hope to die three times over.'

This might have been no more than a conversation between kids, but what they were saying meant that the girl would be here soon.

She'd see me... and the corpse of this priest. I had to do something, and quickly.

Quickly, I started to drag Father Grey's body to the right, towards a point where the wall started to curve around to follow the slight bend in the river. This wouldn't give any real protection to me – the dead man and I would still be readily visible if this little girl, Linda, happened to even so much as glance in our direction – but it was better than nothing.

Father Grey's body was heavy, and the sound of small running feet was getting closer as I dragged his weighty form across the concrete. Fortunately, whoever I was now seemed to be strong, and I managed to complete my task at the exact moment a girl in a dirty pink frock rounded the corner. Pointlessly, I pressed myself closer to the wall.

She looked down at the ground in search of the ball, not seeing it at first. She'd be sure to see me though, if not the crumpled form of Father Grey, if she only lifted her head. Ludicrously, I wanted to shout, *'It's there! It's there just behind you! Look!'*

I have to confess that for a moment I had the desperate idea of emerging from my inadequate hiding place and throwing the girl bodily in the river. But I knew I could never do such a wicked thing. What would I do when Keith came running over from behind the wall to investigate? Kill him too? Still the fact that I'd even, if only for a moment, had this thought horrified me.

Did it come from the person whose body I was slowly coming to realise I now occupied? What sort of creature was he? I felt sick with horror at the thought.

The seconds ticked by. The young girl would surely spot me trying to flatten myself against the wall.

'Linda! Come on! You're taking ages just to pick up a stupid ball. What's keeping you?'

'Coming!'

With that, Linda turned around swept up the ball and ran off, all as if in one movement. I needed no second invitation as soon as she was out of sight. Leaving Father Grey's body where it was, I hurried away in a downstream direction.

*

It was a raw Winter's day. I had walked about two miles, keeping to the river where I could – this wasn't always possible in 1960.

Back then, the towpath wasn't continuous as it is now. I saw no other people as I trudged along.

Then, as I was approaching one of the bridges, I did at last see someone. He seemed to be taking more interest in me than made me comfortable. The newcomer was a tall, thin man approaching from the opposite direction, dressed untidily in a cap, threadbare overcoat and dark scarf muffled around his ears. As we drew closer, he smiled ingratiatingly.

'Victor!' he called, almost before we had come near enough.

I didn't answer. When we had almost drawn level with each other he spoke again, this time in more normal tones. For some reason, the thin man seemed to be incredibly nervous about our encounter.

'Haven't seen you for ages, mate. Been around the docks on the other side for a few months, me.'

'*Victor*?' Was that my name? My expression must have given my thought away.

'Don't arse around, mate,' he said. 'We've known each other for ages, you and me. Don't try to pull your usual trick with your old chum.'

He smiled anxiously, as if realising he might have spoken too boldly.

'Course, I know you might be calling yourself by one of the other names you like to use round here. You always were a rum 'un with all of them names. Bet your real name's not really Victor, anyway.'

He laughed shortly and forced a wholly unreal smile upon his lips.

So, I must be called Victor, then. Or at least one of the names of the person who had once occupied this body was Victor. The other man was now smiling at me broadly. He seemed to like whoever Victor might have been, although was clearly uneasy in his presence. I decided to risk it and take a chance.

'Sorry, fella; I've had a bit of a bump on the head. My memory has been completely wiped out. I can't even remember the names of either of us.'

Was I saying too much to this man? But what else could I do?

The tall man smiled again, even more nervously this time. He looked at me doubtfully.

'Pull the other one, china.'

'I'm not joking, honestly.' I tried to look as serious as I could. This wasn't hard to do. I was seriously worried.

At first, the other tried to keep smiling, but then his expression slowly changed to one of concern.

'You should get yourself some help, Victor. Have one of the doctors in a hospital to have a look at you. I'll take you to the one near here if you like.'

'Maybe later. You've already told me my name. What's yours?'

'Ernie. You sure you're not pulling my plonker, Victor, are you mate? There's no need for it.'

'I swear.'

'Right. That's settled, then.'

Ernie still looked dubious, as if he were doing no more than going along with an elaborate joke he didn't quite understand.

'Ernie,' I said. 'I want you to do me a big favour now. Tell me everything you know about me.'

'Well, there's a question to ask a chum you've known for years.'

'I mean it. Please tell me all you can.'

This Ernie looked puzzled at my question. He looked down at his dusty shoes, then searched my face.

'Well, it's not so easy, is it?'

'Of course it must be. You've known me for years. You just said so.'

Here, Ernie swept off his cap, revealing a bald pate. He scratched his head theatrically before answering.

'So I did, so I did. I met you first a year or two before the old king died. Not far from here on the riverbank, it was. Since then, I've seen you scores of times, mainly near the river between Putney Bridge and Chelsea Bridge, close to the power station. The river and the streets around it is our beat; neither of us have ever left it, except when I took it into my head to try The Island for a change last October.'

Now it was my turn to be puzzled. Exactly where was this island he was talking about?

'But surely, I must have told you something more in all that time? It's nearly eight years since King George went.' Somehow, I knew this, even though I had no idea what my own name was before Ernic told me.

'Not really mate,' said Ernie, resettling his cap more comfortably on his head. 'Before the war you lived in Birmingham or somewhere like that. Your name – the name you've always used with me, anyway, is Victor Smith. That's about all I can tell you. Oh, and this is your usual beat, of course.'

Smith... war... something was twitching around the edge of my memory.

'Was I in the war, Ernie?'

'Course you were, Victor. Most of the blokes around our age were. You were in the army, like me. You never said anything about it, though. I couldn't even tell you what regiment you were in. You never said.'

'Nothing? I said nothing?'

'Couldn't tell you another thing,' said Ernie. 'Now, we really ought to get going to that hospital. I wouldn't wait if I were you, mate.'

The last thing I dared do was to have any kind of contact with officialdom: doctors, police, anyone really. I'd left a dead man a short distance downriver.

'Can't do that, Ernie. Fact is, I'm in trouble.'

He laughed. He laughed in my face.

'You're always in trouble, Victor! You've been up in front of the beak loads of times, mate.'

'I mean *big* trouble.'

Ernie took his cap off again. This time, he didn't scratch his head.

'You were always talking about pulling a big job. So now you've gone and done it, eh? But doctors aren't like the law, you know. A cosy chat with one of them and a square meal in hospital would be the exact thing for you. If you play your cards right a hospital might be a good place to lie low for a bit, too.'

'I think I need to lie a bit lower than that. It's not a robbery they'll be after me for. It's something worse.'

He looked at me with wonder. Then his eyes were crossed by a mixture of emotions: horror, awe, respect and, finally, a resurgence of his fear.

'You mean... Who? Where? No, don't tell me. I don't want to know.'

'Where can I lie low for a bit?'

I asked this question because the only places I somehow knew at the fringe of my memory were North Ruislip and Parva-vale. I could hardly run to either of them.

'Nowhere around here, mate.' I could see Ernie now wanted to get out of my company as soon as he could. 'Get yourself onto The Island. That's my advice. It's not a wonderful place to be but nobody knows you there. People don't ask questions.'

'The Island? There's no island around here.'

'Yes, there is. Poplar and Millwall. Go somewhere around there. Folk there are great. It's different to the rest of London, The Island is. I'll tell you how to get there if you like.'

*

That last car was the fourth police Anglia to pass by this bus stop. I thought every one of them would be out looking for me, but in each case the driver and front-seat passenger firmly kept their eyes on the road ahead.

Ernie had been relieved to learn I did propose to travel to the place he'd recommended, 'The Island', as he called it. I'd been wondering whether to make the journey by bus rather than by continuing to slog along the Thames bank on foot. Something even as everyday as a bus the Victor within me seemed to regard as somehow 'official'. He was a strange man, as well as being an unpleasant one.

But when Ernie had told me Millwall wasn't far off ten miles away, I remembered Father Grey's wallet in my pocket. My decision was made, regardless of Victor's reluctance.

According to Ernie, who had seemed far from certain, the first bus I was supposed to catch was a number eleven to Liverpool Street. This was already further east than I'd ever travelled before. I'd had a fair walk to this bus stop from the river, so I considered it to be money well spent. Anyway, the money had fallen into my hands. In a manner of speaking it had, anyway.

When the bus turned up I, the only one waiting at the stop on this cold Friday morning – somehow, I knew it was Friday – stuck my hand out, feeling almost as if I was about to embark on a voyage of discovery. I climbed up the stairs proudly. This feeling didn't last for long.

'Fares please!'

The bus conductor strutted along the upper-deck aisle towards me. He was clearly annoyed at having to climb the stairs because one of his few passengers had for no good reason chosen to ride on the upper deck.

It was at that moment I remembered: there were only notes in Father Grey's wallet. Hesitantly, I pulled the expensive leather object from my pocket, once again admiring its neat stitching. Luckily, my fingers fell upon the single green oncer among at least a dozen big white fivers. There wasn't even a ten-bob note.

This priest, whatever else he might have been, must have been loaded. Gingerly, I fished out the pound note and handed it to the conductor.

'Liverpool Street station, please.'

'What do you call this?'

'That's the money for my bus fare.'

He snorted derisively.

'And you've got the nerve to give me all this? What do you think I am – a bank? I've only just come on shift. Give me something smaller, mate.'

'It's all I have. Look.'

I opened my wallet to show him. Big mistake. He saw all those lovely white fivers.

'You've half-inched these, haven't you, you little sod? Tramp like you doesn't have a fancy wallet of his own stuffed full of fivers. I'm going to get the law on to you.'

With that he sprang away from me and shouted, 'STOP THE BUS! THIEF ON THE

BUS'. He could have pulled the cable twice or whatever it was they were supposed to do, but the driver must have heard him, anyway – as would have everyone else within half a mile. Soon the bus was screeching to a halt.

The conductor, a short man in early middle age, stepped forward as if to seize my arm. I have to admit, I panicked at that moment. I didn't want to have anything to do with the police, especially when I was in the possession of the wallet of a man who had died – probably at my hand, even though I still couldn't remember anything like this happening – only that same morning.

I leaped up from my seat, knocking the surprised conductor backwards. He fell into a seat and from there rolled into the aisle. I jumped awkwardly over his cursing form and raced down the stairs.

I hurled myself from the platform of the stationary bus and hared off down Tommy Bridge Road, as I saw its name was. I didn't once look behind me to see if anyone from the bus was giving chase. Fortunately, I saw no policemen, either.

If this had been a pedestrian bridge, I'd have raced across to the other side. As it was, I found some steps down to the river a bit further along and, once I was standing on its bank, drew in gasps of air. I started to feel some security down by the river. It was strange: the Thames had never been important in my life before now.

Wait a moment: how did I know a thing like that? Slowly, odd things started to come together in my addled brain. Until late November, I'd lived a dull life as young Steve Charles. So why on Earth was I now in the body of this odd, aggressive little man? Where did the priest, Father Grey – somehow, I knew this was his name – come into the picture? Had I really murdered him for the fat leather wallet now in my pocket?

My head reeled. It was all too much to take in. Somehow, Goodness knows how, I managed to stumble on downriver for a few miles more. Then, I simply had to look for somewhere to rest. It was too early to sleep, so I tucked myself away behind some statue adorned with ancient pigeon droppings as best I could. Then I tried to make some sense of what was happening to me.

Father Grey was the man whose body I had stood over in Wandsworth and whose wallet was in my pocket now. Had I really killed him for his wallet and had his being – or Steve Charles's being – taken over the body of this Victor Smith? The name drifted again into my mind, along with several other aliases he used. Another name that came unbidden into my dazed mind was Jim Corcoran. Exactly who was he and where did he fit into the picture?

As I lay there, as if on some nauseating roundabout, more of the details started to piece together. Victor *hadn't* killed the priest. Father Grey was a sick man. Victor had simply happened to be on the spot at the moment of the priest's death.

The priest's spirit – or that of Steve Charles – had taken over the body of Victor Smith. No, not quite spirit, *Ka* was the word. I now remembered reading a book on the subject in Wandsworth Prison, when I was in the body of Jim Corcoran. In the body of Jim Corcoran?

*

'Oi you! Wake up! You can't sleep there, mate. This is a respectable part of London.'

A policeman was shaking my shoulder roughly. I slowly started to come to. What was I doing here now? Where exactly was 'here'? As I scrambled dazedly to my feet, I saw the Houses of Parliament on the other side of the river. Then I remembered.

Yesterday I was in such a state that I couldn't walk as far as I'd planned. I'd intended to press on to my destination, but I had to stop and try to sort my confused thoughts out. I'd spent the night in another hidey-hole I'd found near Lambeth Bridge, but it seemed it wasn't so easy to stay out of the reach of authority figures.

'Sorry, officer,' I said. 'I'm on the way to the Isle of Dogs.'

'You've got a walk ahead of you, then. Get going and make sure I don't see you anywhere on my beat again.'

I slunk along the riverbank feeling his eyes boring between my shoulder-blades. But it wasn't that troubling me. Last night I had somehow managed to piece the details of my life together, from a drab existence as a young Steve Charles to brief, unhappy occupations of the bodies of Jim Corcoran and Father Hubert Grey. Now it was a similar story with Victor Smith, an aimless, thoroughly nasty, down-and-out.

So far, Victor Smith, exactly as Jim Corcoran had in the priest's, seemed to leave few traces of his essence in this body. I, Steve Charles, thought I'd at least have sole possession of a body this time. How wrong I was.

*

The further east I walked; the more bomb damage was in evidence. You'd think, nearly fifteen years after the war, most of it would have been cleared up by now, but this was plainly not so. Here in Millwall, going by all the noise and cranes, even on a Sunday, some sort of start toward reconstruction seemed to be in progress, but plainly there was a long way to go.

Saturday night I'd spent in a chilly nook close to the river, where I'd been awoken by a cold mist creeping from the water and feeling as though it was entering my bones.

It had been exactly the same story the night before, Friday. I couldn't see any alternative to repeating the experience tonight. All I'd had to eat yesterday was half a cold pie given to me by a fellow – let's face it – tramp. This morning I was ravenously hungry as well as thirsty. Here, there didn't even seem to be the drinking fountains that had been so easy to find in the parks of Central London.

There was nothing else for it. I'd have to risk it and walk into a fish-and-chip shop or anywhere else I could find open on a Sunday morning. Then I'd have pay for the food with my single pound note. I'd make sure no one would catch sight of all those fivers in my wallet again. I could have a whole bottle of fizzy lemonade for myself, too, if that was what I fancied.

I began to warm to this plan. Even if all I got was a polite or not-so-polite refusal to accept payment by banknote, this time it would surely be accompanied by no more than a suspiciously raised eyebrow, if a pound note was all I could produce.

Looking up and down the street to make sure there was no-one in sight, I pulled out Father Grey's wallet and hunched over it, as if I'd stolen it. I suppose, in a way, this was exactly what I had done. It looked to be an expensive one, with its soft, pinkish leather and an embossed 'HG' on the outside corner. I counted out seventy pounds, all in white fivers. Strange. Where was the pound note?

Then I remembered. The last time I'd seen the money, it was clenched in the fist of the conductor of the number eleven bus in his surprised sprawl on the upper-deck gangway of his vehicle.

'Excuse me.'

A man rounded the corner of the side street near to me and I accosted him.

'Yes?'

I, or Steve Charles anyway, don't normally address strangers so boldly, but I was becoming desperate. He had a friendly face. I suppose it was this that encouraged me.

'Can you tell me where I can find something to eat?'

'Well, there's a chippy around that Johnny Horner, but it's shut up shop this week.' He looked at me doubtfully, clearly wondering if I was looking for some sort of handout. 'Or there's a charity place about a mile further down the shake and shiver. It's a left in the bleedin' lurch thing, though, so I don't know how they'd be fixed on a Sunday. They'll probably be off bowin' an' prayin' somewhere.'

'I'm not looking for charity,' I said, trying to assume an air of hurt pride. In fact, I'd have taken a handout readily to stop this gnawing feeling in my guts, even though I knew I had more than enough to pay for what I wanted. An idea came to me. 'Maybe somewhere that does board and lodge?'

His look changed from one of doubt to one of pity.

'Well, me and the Missus have a spare va-va-voom now the kids have gone and our lodger suddenly upped and left us last week. Good thing we'd charged two nicker a week in advance. We'd want a oncer deposit… I'm not just saying that to you… It'd be the same thing for anyone. Wouldn't it be better if I told you where to find the church place?'

'I'll take your room.'

He looked at me in disbelief. It was a long moment before he spoke.

'Not being funny, mate, but the trouble and strife wouldn't be happy if I take you home with me in that sort of two and eight. Sorry. Really sorry.'

He looked genuinely sorry, too. I could understand his reservations.

'It's OK, I'm not offended. Long story why I'm dressed like this.' And I wasn't going to tell the story, or even try to make one up. 'Do you know anywhere I could get some decent clobber on a Sunday?'

He doubled up with laughter when I said this.

'Well, ain't you a rum 'un. You want some in the nude, an Uncle Ned and now a Sinbad the Sailor. Anyway, your Donald Duck is in, mate. Someone I know is selling off a whistle and flute and some other stuff. Left after a cousin who'd bought it, the gear was. But, before we go any further, don't you think you should show me the colour of your bangers an' mash?'

'What?

I looked at him blankly. I was having a lot of trouble understanding what he was saying.

'Your cash, bread and honey, money.'

It was a reasonable thing to ask, but how was I to do it without showing him I was carrying so much money? I turned my back to him.

'Just a minute.' I opened Father Grey's wallet. With unsteady hands I extracted a single five-pound note. Then, more clumsily than I'd have liked, I turned around and handed it to him.

'Christ! A deep-sea diver! I don't want all this.'

I thought quickly.

'It's two weeks rent and the deposit you wanted.'

He held the banknote up, examining it as if he'd never seen one before.

'Where did you get so much bread and honey?'

'I won it in a bet. That's why I'm dressed like this. Long story, like I told you.'

'Well, aren't you going to tell me this Jackanory?'

'Not now. Haven't got time, have we? I'll tell you when I can.'

And perhaps when I'd been able to make some sort of story up.

'Suppose you're right. We'll go and see George now. He used to work in a bank, so he can tell me if this deep-sea diver is a wrong 'un while we're at it.'

Father Grey carrying forged banknotes? Surely not. But I was nervous as I followed my new friend back around the corner.

'What's your name?' I called after him. 'Mine's... Victor.'

He stopped in his tracks, turned around to face me then shook me warmly by the hand.

''Eaven and 'ell chuffed to meet you, Victor. Me own moniker is Tommy. Georgie Porgy isn't far away. Just around the other field of wheat down there and we'll be at his Dorothy Lamour.'

*

I'd fallen on my feet. Not only did George have a suit to sell me, but also a shirt, overcoat, and a more-or-less presentable tie. The lot was nineteen shillings and sixpence, paid for by Tommy out of the pound 'deposit' I'd left with him. George had even given me two sets of underclothes and socks of his own. Fortunately, the old shoes I wore were almost presentable. I was glad to get out of Victor's grubby things and relieved when Tommy offered to get George to burn them.

'It's only a few streets away to mine. Jean will be surprised to see who's coming to dinner,' said Tommy. 'Come on.'

*

Jean wasn't too alarmed to see Tommy bringing a surprise dinner guest and lodger home with him. It seemed he'd done this sort of thing before. She was a smart redhead, probably a few years younger than her husband.

She greeted me with a winning smile and welcoming words. I wish she hadn't been such a good-looking woman. I'm sure it was her attraction that first stirred Victor's true essence from the safety of its slumber.

'Take Victor up to his room, Tommy. He can sort himself out before dinner. We'll be eating in an hour. It's roast lamb for us this week. Your favourite, Tommy.'

My 'sorting out' consisted of nothing more than pushing the spare underclothes and socks into the top drawer of the old dressing table. Besides the single bed, an empty wardrobe, a rickety wooden chair and a nondescript, unframed sketch of a country scene on the otherwise plain wall, this was all the room contained.

I studied my reflection in the dressing table mirror. Victor's appearance had been vastly improved by the new clothes. It still needed trimming but even his beard now seemed to have some style, rather than being nothing more than an unshaven mess. The man had been almost good-looking, in a rough-edged sort of way.

Victor looked back at me and smiled. This is no mere figure of speech. For that single moment he, rather than me as Steve Charles, had taken possession of his own body.

I shook my head and looked again into the eyes staring back at me from the mirror. They were grey rather than the hazel I'd been used to in North Ruislip, but I knew they were once again a window to my own confused soul, rather than what I was to discover to be the sinister one of Victor Smith.

*

'Take more lamb if you want it, Victor,' said Jean. 'There's plenty there for the three of us.'

There was indeed plenty. More than that. Besides the piles of sliced meat, there were tureens overflowing with monstrous potatoes, runner beans, peas, and carrots. There were two overfilled gravy boats and a huge glass jar holding what I was told was 'sauce made with fresh mint from Tommy's patch in the yard'.

Jean herself made considerable inroads into all this food. Tommy consumed at least twice as much as his wife. It was clear from the couple's constant urging that I was expected to eat at least a third of the food in front of me. I was full before even the first of the dishes of potatoes was half-empty.

'I expect you like lots of skin on your rice pudding, don't you, Victor?'

As soon as I politely could, I excused myself from the post prandial living room. I went upstairs to sleep off the biggest meal I'd eaten in my life. Only hours before I'd been near to starving.

*

Sunday evening was structured around a viewing of *Sunday Night at the London*

Palladium, a variety show whose theme music I'd often heard through the front room door of my lodgings in North Ruislip, although I'd never once been invited in to watch the television.

'This Forsyth bloke will never be as good as good old Tommy Trinder,' said Tommy.

'You say that every week,' said Jean. 'He's not at all bad, this new bloke. What do you think, Victor?'

'I… um… um… they're both OK by me.'

I hardly knew either name. Tommy Trinder used to be on the radio, and I thought was the Chairman of Fulham Football Club. This for some reason I had identified years before as 'my team'. The 'new bloke' was no more than a name to me. I had no opinion on the merits of either man in the role of compere of a variety show I'd never before seen.

But, as she'd turned around in her chair to speak to me, Jean's happy face had been lit up pleasingly and her full breasts had bobbed invitingly underneath their thin covering of the yellow flowered dress she wore. I, Steve Charles, thought she was attractive. But then I felt a sudden convulsion passing through me. Victor was stirring.

'Do you mind if I turn in early tonight?' I said. 'It's been a long day for me.'

'You haven't told me about the bet you made yet,' said Tommy. 'You know, how you came to be dressed like a tramp when I met you in Acris Street. Got to be a good story I can tell the blokes on the dock in there somewhere.'

'Come on, Tommy,' said Jean. 'We can both hear all about it tomorrow when you come home from work. Let Victor climb the silken stair in peace. Usual time for you?'

'No overtime this week. We're a bit quiet.'

It was only thirty minutes after I'd turned in that I heard Tommy ascending the staircase outside my bedroom. Fifteen minutes after that came Jean's lighter tread. I heard the muffled tones of the couple's lovemaking through the bedroom wall. Then all became silent. They must have dropped off quickly. But it was hours later before I managed get any sleep myself. Victor wouldn't let me rest.

*

'Three rashers or four? Two or three eggs? I've got some nice black pudding this morning – it'll be exactly right with fried bread.

'Only one egg and two rashers, please, Jean. No black pudding, thanks. Aren't you eating anything yourself?'

'Had mine with Tommy an hour ago.'

Jean retreated from what was grandly called 'The Dining Room' into the tiny cubby hole of a kitchen. I could still see her bustling about through the open hatchway. I wished I couldn't see her. Or, rather, I wish Victor Smith hadn't been able to see her. I could feel animal desires rising within his body.

They were fast welling up, like some physical entity, urging me to get up from the table and go to her in the small kitchen. Beyond this, I had no plan. In fact, there was nothing you could describe as consciousness involved in what I did next.

At all events, before I knew it, I found myself standing at the kitchen door. Jean hadn't heard me. She was absorbed in her task of slicing the black pudding on the chopping-board before her.

I stepped forward silently and, in one movement, cupped my hand about her full breasts and eased myself against her soft curves. Immediately, I felt her body stiffen.

'Jean, I…'

She wriggled. It was lovely. For a moment I, Steve Charles, really knew what it must have been like to be Victor. But then she brought her elbow sharply back into my ribs. I had to loosen my hold and step back. She struggled to turn around and face me.

'Get away, you filthy animal!'

'I've got sixty-five pounds in my pocket. It can be all yours if you let me have my way with you for an hour… half an hour.'

The words came tumbling out of my mouth. I – Steve Charles – had no experience with women, but even as I heard the words coming unbidden from my own mouth, I knew it was entirely the wrong thing for anyone to say.

Jean didn't answer directly. How could she? Instead, her eyes widened, and she unleashed a terrified scream. At that moment, the door from the passageway into the dining room opened. He stood there. Tommy.

'What's going on here?'

'Oh, Tommy!' said Jean. 'I'm so glad to see you. This man attacked me! Just like that. One minute he was sitting at the table while I was getting his breakfast ready. The next he had those filthy hands on me and was pressing…'

Tommy stepped forward. I could see he was prepared to rip my head off. I knew Victor was sturdy, but Tommy was so much taller and heavily muscled, into the bargain. It would have been no real contest. Then – why she did it I don't know, but I am grateful that she did – Jean stepped in between us.

'No, Tommy. He's not worth it. You'll only be in more trouble if you hurt someone badly again.'

Tommy glowered at me but stepped back a pace.

'It's as well for you there was no work on the docks for me today. We give him a meal and a good bed, and this is how he repays us. I've a mind to…'

Jean stepped forward again.

'NO! Just throw him out. Do it as hard as you like, but don't leave any marks he can show to the police.'

Tommy needed no second invitation. Before I knew it, I was being half-carried – at least, that's what it felt like – down the short passageway. Then I was bodily thrown out into the gutter. At least, the lower half of my sprawled form ended up in the road and my head lay on a broken paving stone.

At first, seeing it from eyes only inches from its surface, I really thought it had broken in contact with my head. Then I realised the crack on the surface must have been old damage. I was dazed more with shock than feeling much in the way of real physical pain.

The front door was slammed shut. I struggled to a seated position next to a downpipe. It was only then I realised it was raining steadily. Confused, I tried to assess my position.

Now I'd lost the jacket and overcoat I'd gained only yesterday. It was wet and cold. I'd had no breakfast. Despite the stupendous meal I'd eaten only yesterday, I was already beginning to grow hungry.

There were still a dozen or so Fivers in the wallet in the pocket of my trousers, but I knew I dared not try to spend them. I knew the Victor within me would never allow me to walk into a shop.

My stay in Millwall had cost me a Fiver – the four pounds I'd given to Tommy and the pound I'd spent on clothes, the more important of which I no longer possessed. All right, in theory I'd only spent nineteen shillings and sixpence with George, but I could hardly knock at Tommy's front door and ask for my Tanner back.

Suddenly, this door opened. Tommy stood there, threateningly. I flinched away, thinking he'd won the argument with Jean and was coming to lay into me.

'You still here? Jean says I was to give you this.'

He flung the jacket and overcoat he'd been holding behind his back into a small puddle on the pavement next to my right hand.

'And take these, too. We don't want any of your filthy money in this house.'

He floated four Oncers to the ground. I dared not look up to see where they landed.

'And this is from me personally, you little shit! You left it upstairs.'

He flung something at my head. I closed my eyes and felt a small, hard object zinging against the tip of my right ear.

I was afraid to open my eyes until I heard the front door close. When at last it did I tilted my head back to see what Tommy had thrown at me. I saw it was a small shiny coin. A sixpenny piece.

*

Half of the sixpence meant I could treat myself to a hot dog for my Monday lunch. I couldn't resist another a few hours later, even if this meant I could see no alternative to spending a chilly night in the open near Garnet Street in Wapping. Here I also managed to beg a few chips from a passing youth.

I was afraid to venture into Central London, fearing another encounter with the forces of law and order. Some irrational fear – it must have been Victor's influence again – prevented me from taking the sensible step of walking into a bank and cashing one of the banknotes in the wallet lying uselessly in my pocket.

On Tuesday morning, I did at last summon up the courage to strike out and walked westward, all the way into the heart of the city. Now that I was better dressed, everyone ignored me, including the only two constables I saw.

But I couldn't find a thing for breakfast, beyond a drink from a water fountain in one of the parks. Back on the riverbank, just as Big Ben was striking the hour at two o'clock, my luck changed briefly. I found a whole shilling bit.

This, together with a bit of outright begging and the stealing of bread and scraps meant for the pigeons and ducks, was enough to keep me alive for the next three days. But it felt like I was only just alive. I started to see more bobbies out on the prowl and spent much of my time making long detours to avoid them. Finally, on Thursday morning, I resolved to head towards the place where this unhappy life had, in a way, begun. It was hard to believe this was less than a week ago.

*

Why I made this decision I'm still not sure. There might be fewer blue uniforms to be seen further west, but they could still be looking for someone – they might even be looking for me – in connection with the death of Father Grey. Now I knew I, as Stephen Charles, that neither Victor Smith, nor anyone else, hadn't killed him. But what might others be thinking?

The priest was, after all, an extremely sick man. Nobody knew this better – I knew it from the inside. If I was apprehended, I'd tell the truth. This was what I'd resolved to do. Not the whole truth, of course – I'd just say I'd seen him die and had been frightened enough to flee to the other side of London. Some sort of inquest would surely bear out the fact that when I was telling them he'd died from natural causes. I'd be telling the truth.

The snag with this plan was that I was still carrying Father Grey's cash and wallet in my pocket. I knew the sensible thing would be to throw the lot in the river. I found it impossible to bring myself to do a thing like that. Perhaps, if I kept the four one-pound notes, or even just a few of them, I might be able to do it. At the very least, if I could pluck up the courage to walk in somewhere and buy one, I should then be able to buy myself a decent meal before I did the deed.

What had my life become? Where was I going? Was my new existence to consist of nothing more than aimless, half-starved wanderings up and down London's river? Would I always have to keep an eye out for blue uniforms?

It was while I was thinking about these things that I saw him. Or, rather, we saw each other at the same instant. He hurried towards me.

'Victor!' He greeted me like a friend. Perhaps he was the nearest thing Victor had to a friend. 'Fancy seeing you here again. You couldn't have spent much time on The Island. It was less than a week ago when I saw you.'

'No, Ernie. It didn't work out.'

He laughed shortly.

'Well, you've missed all the excitement around here. There was a murder. At least, everyone thought at first there'd been a murder. I was worried about what you'd told me on that morning I saw you, I don't mind saying. I thought you'd been involved – well, anybody would after the things you'd said.'

This was awkward. I'd told Ernie a lot more than I should have last Friday.

'Sorry, old friend. It was part of the effect of the bump on the head I'd had that morning. I even lost my memory, like I told you. Still, everything's tickety-boo now.'

'Even for that driver, eh?'

Who was Ernie talking about? What driver?

'I don't follow you there Ernie, mate.'

'I was forgetting for a minute – you weren't around when the story came out. You'd have been on The Island by then, wouldn't you?'

Ernie wasn't making any sense to me. This must have showed on my face because he quickly continued with his story. I could see he thought I really already knew it, nevertheless.

'Well, they found the body of this old priest down by the river. It was two kids playing cricket who found the geezer. Dead as a doornail, the old man was.'

'Well, I'll say this for the Rozzers – they didn't waste any time in nabbing that driver.'

Ernie was clearly expecting me to say something, but I held my silence. He continued:

'Turns out someone had seen this bloke taking the old priest down to the river in a big car. Well, that's not a thing you'd be doing unless you've got something murky in mind, is it? Anyway, for some reason he drives back to the river later, pretending he was looking for the priest. That was when they arrested him.'

Ken… Ernie could only be talking about Ken.

'What was the driver's name? Do you know?'

'Course I know. Ken Barker, his name is. Everyone's been following the story. That was easy, what with all the Rozzers around – and some proper detectives, too. Asking questions of all and sundry, they were. They even pulled me in. Don't worry, mate. I never said anything about you. You know I never would.'

Here Ernie looked at me searchingly. There was more than a hint of suspicion in his eyes.

'Why should that matter, Ernie? I've told you about the crack on my head.'

'Yes, but when you old me that you'd only just said you'd been mixed up in some bad stuff and… oh, it doesn't matter now, does it?'

Ernie shuffled his feet restlessly. He clearly wanted to be on his way.

'What were you going to say, Ern? Tell me.'

He wouldn't answer and looked at the ground.

'Come on. Tell me.'

'It's probably nothing.' Ernie was clearly resentful about having whatever it was dragged out of him. 'He might have spoken to you earlier or something like that. I don't know, do I?'

'It could be important. Let me decide whether it's nothing.'

Who was this 'he' Ernie was talking about?

'Oh, it's just that when this driver – this Ken Barker – was grabbed by the cops he was protesting that Father Grey had gone to see someone called "Victor". He was the one they should be looking for, Kenny boy told them. He said he hadn't met you himself, so couldn't even describe you. This must have sounded a bit thin to the boys in blue.'

It didn't sound thin to me.

'So, what did the police do then?'

'Well, give them their due. They asked around about "Victor". Of course, nobody thought of you, so they drew a blank. They all know you as "Johnnie" or "Frank" by this part of the river. Everyone does except me. And Mavis, of course.'

Who was Mavis?

'Did they speak to you about me? What did you say?'

'They spoke to me. Of course, they did. You don't think I'm one to start telling stories to the Rozzers, do you? I haven't seen Mavis since then, but I know she wouldn't have said anything either, even if you're not her favourite person.'

He laughed when he said this. It was clear that Victor was a long way from being Mavis's favourite.

'Well, what happened then?' I said.

'Well, things looked bad for Kenny boy, didn't they? An open-and-shut case if there ever was one. They even checked with the old priest's housekeeper, is what I heard – some old tart called Mrs Broadbent – but all she could tell them is that the priest and Kenny went off on some hush-hush mission last Friday. Neither of them would say a word about where they were going, or why, to her.'

Poor Ken! Through no fault of his own, he'd become the chief suspect in a murder case. The irony was, there hadn't even been a murder. I was reminded of the parallels with Jim Corcoran's story.

'Tell me, what happened then?'

Ernie still looked at me with something more than a ghost of suspicion in his eyes. He was clearly sure that I knew a lot more than I was letting on.

'Like I say, things looked black for the driver. But then someone from Jews' Row came forward and said they'd seen him dropping the priest off through the window. He was safe and sound then. After that, others said they'd seen the same thing. You don't get many big cars like that one in Jews' Row now, do you?'

Ernie clearly wanted to cease his account there and be on his way, but I beckoned him with an impatient hand signal to continue.

'So, they did a second post-mortem – lazy bastards, they should have done a proper job to start with. This time, they said the old man had died from natural causes. His own doctor said he had a dickie heart. You'd have thought they'd have asked him before then. Yesterday they had to let the driver go. All's well that ends well, eh?'

But Ernie's expression belied his words. I pressed him on the subject.

'There's still something you're not happy about with all this, is there, mate?'

It didn't at first look as if Ernie wanted to say more. When he spoke, the words were laden with suspicion.

'The driver was in the clear, yes. But why was he talking about a 'Victor'? No one knows that's your name.'

I thought quickly.

'It's like you said, Ern. I spoke to this Ken just before he drove off. He knows my name is Victor.'

This wasn't exactly a lie. I had indeed spoken to Ken. But I was then occupying the body of Father Grey. There were other loose ends, too. Surely Victor wouldn't have told Ken his real name? Why hadn't others in Jews' Row reported seeing Victor, even if they didn't know him by any name? What was this crack on the head I'd told him about? No wonder there was mystification and doubt written all over Ernie's features.

'Oh, I see.' Really, he could see nothing.

It was clear to me that Ernie couldn't tell me anything else of value.

'Well, can't spend all day chewing the fat with you,' I said. 'I'm off.'

Ernie looked relieved to be released from this unwanted conversation, smiled nervously, and started to walk away.

'Bye, mate,' he said, barely turning his head as he passed me.

I'd have liked to have found out more about Mavis, the only other who apparently knew anything about Victor. Clearly, I couldn't have prolonged this conversation much longer. Besides, how could I put the sort of questions I wanted answered to Ernie? Victor was supposed to know her himself. I could hardly pull the memory-loss stunt again.

Who was Mavis? Less than half-an-hour later, I was to meet her myself.

*

I was walking a few hundred yards west of Wandsworth Bridge. In those days, there was no proper towpath all the way. It wasn't possible to keep to the river all the way along. I was cutting across some long-grassed waste ground not far from the river when I saw her.

The only sights to be seen were two rusting bike frames and a pile of abandoned milk crates. My sole thoughts were whether I'd manage to find somewhere in Putney to spend the night and if I dared to, with my new tidied-up appearance, whether I'd be able to ignore Victor's strange influence enough to go into a shop with a One Pound note.

Suddenly, I became aware of a woman coming towards me from the other direction. She didn't notice me at first. When she did, it was clear from her expression that I was the last person she'd have wished to meet. But there was now no way for her to avoid me.

For a second, I thought she seemed oddly familiar, but I soon decided I was in error. She herself would have thought she was seeing Victor, anyway.

'Victor!' she cried when she was near enough to me. Her greeting may have been friendly enough, but she didn't seem in the least pleased to see me.

This could only be Mavis. Ernie had said she was the only other one who knew Victor by that name.

'Mavis. How good to see you.'

She looked surprised at the seeming warmth of my greeting. In fact, the last thing I wanted was to waste time with another down-and-out. This is what she clearly was, with her torn carrier bag and general forlorn appearance. She looked about sixty years of age, though now I'm sure this was probably superficial, a factor of her hard lifestyle.

'Wish I could say the same, Victor. I don't want any trouble. Not like last time. I didn't say anything to the police about you, I swear.'

The police? Was she talking about the same thing as Ernie had just now? Somehow, I didn't think she was.

'Mavis, I-'. I didn't know what I was going to say. It didn't matter, anyway, because I could feel a powerful force rising within me. Victor's own essence was taking control of his body again... By the look of her, she could see the change in my expression and was growing nervous.

'Let me pass, please, Victor. I want no trouble.'

'Don't be so hasty, Mavis. Be nice to your old friend for once.'

'Leave me be. I remember what you did last time I was on my own with you.'

'Look, I've got a quid for you.'

'Go away! Leave me alone.'

She looked nervously about her. There was no one in sight. I took my wallet – Father Grey's wallet – from my pocket and waved a note at her.

'A whole quid, Mavis. Think about it. You usually do it for five bob. Less sometimes, so I've heard.' This was what I said. But I didn't think the thought behind the words. Victor was claimed full repossession, exactly as he'd done last Monday morning in that kitchen in Millwall.

Mavis tried to scream, but only a strangled gurgle came from her mouth.

'Shut up, woman! D'you want to bring the law around here or something? Squawking like a parrot, you are.'

I – Victor – launched myself at Mavis. I caught her by both legs, and she fell heavily on her face.

'You're going to pay for this,' I said. 'And you can forget the quid. You can forget the five bob, come to that. I don't like being messed about by an old tart.'

Mavis struggled to roll over onto her back. Then her features softened.

'OK Victor. You win. It won't cost you a thing.'

She started to lift her ragged skirt.

'How do you know that's what I want?'

'Anything you want, Victor. Let's start with the normal though, shall we?'

Now it was my – Victor's – turn to let loose a strangled cry. I – he – leaped upon her.

'Now we…'

Something was wrong. As I wriggled to get better purchase upon her body, I felt a sharp pain in my side. Then another… then another.

'This is all you're going to get from me, Victor. I've been carrying this around in my bag in case we bumped into each other again.'

The sharp pains travelled from my side to my back. As her hand moved towards my throat, I could see the glint of metal in her hand. Mavis had a small stiletto. She was wielding it with fear and anger. Hatred, even. I tried to move but couldn't. Again and again, the knife found its mark. Once more I felt a life force dribbling away from me, this time slowly and painfully.

[5] Mavis

I was thrusting a neat, silver-coloured knife again and again into the bloodied corpse lying next to me upon the ground. The knife was small, but each of the thrusts buried its blade in smoothly and to the hilt. This weapon was sharp

At first, I couldn't stop myself from repeating this gory action. Then, horrified at what I found myself doing, I scrambled to my feet and surveyed my gruesome handiwork. I felt cold.

This time, most of my wits seemed to reassemble all at once as soon as I rose. Despite the grubby female apparel I was wearing, I was really Steve Charles, a young man who, until the end of last November, had been drudging his life away in a wallpaper factory. My only regular leisure had been a weekly card school with some workmates. In truth, this was something I never enjoyed, except for the last evening – part of it, at least.

All had gone well on that final session of cards until it had ended in a freak accident, which resulted not exactly in my death, but in the transfer of something called a Ka to an unfortunate man called Jim Corcoran.

Jim had been hanged for my supposed murder, wherupon this mysterious Ka had moved on to a sick old priest called Father Hubert Grey. In his body I or this Ka had survived for less than a week before moving on for another short period into the body of an unpleasant down-and-out who called himself, among other things, Victor Smith.

His was the mangled corpse lying before me. I knew I hated this man. Which of us truly felt this hate, Steve or the one who'd occupied this body before me, a woman called Mavis? Somehow, I knew the answer to be *both*, although perhaps Mavis loathed him with the greater intensity.

But, as for Mavis, who was she? I did not know. She was clearly also some sort of vagrant. This time, there could be no doubt who was responsible for yet another death. It was Mavis – she was in the act of actually stabbing this Victor at the moment of transfer.

He'd attacked her, yes, but I knew the murder had been committed for other reasons and it was premeditated. I could sense Mavis's satifaction. I had real no idea as to what her motives could have been. Even so I, Steve, still felt a strong wave of sympathy, even protectiveness, towards the woman Mavis.

This was my fifth life in not much more than two months! I could not go on existing like this. I resolved to try to do something about it.

But what should I do? What I *could* do about it was a question that had no answer. More immediately, I now had this bloody crime on my hands. The first thing I had to do was find a way of dealing with the desperate straits.

I was covered in blood from head to foot. It was dripping from my fingertips as I looked down at the dead Victor. What should I do? There might be someone along on this path at any moment. I knew money might somehow help. I also knew Victor Smith was in possession of Father Grey's wallet, so reached inside his coat for it.

'Mavis!'

I felt numbly cold as I heard the call and spun around to see to whom the voice belonged.

There was a man, quite old, standing at the edge of the waste ground. His expression was one of extreme horror. He began cautiously to walk towards me. Was this an act of courage? Or one of foolhardiness? I had, in the old expression, been caught red-handed. I gripped the handle of the small knife tightly…

*

'Feeling any better now after your bath?'

'Yes, thank you, Sir.' Who was he?

'Why on Earth are you calling me Sir? What's wrong with Charlie?'

'Thank you, Charlie.'

This man, this Charlie, looked down at the paper bag containing my clothes and shook his head.

'I'll have to burn all this stuff of yours. It's the only safe way. The trouble is, what can you wear instead? You can hardly go out in that old pair of pyjamas and dressing gown. I've got plenty of other things here, but these days it's all men's clobber.'

He bent his head, almost as if in apology. I could see Charlie was even older than I'd first thought.

'Suppose I could pop out to the second-hand shop around the corner and see what I can pick up. Trouble is, I have no money. Pension day's not until tomorrow...'

'I have money. How much do you need?

'A pound maybe. Two would be better. But you could never...'

My impulse was to snatch Father Grey's wallet from the pocket of the too-large dressing gown I now wore and to thrust one of the fivers into the old man's hand. Then I remembered the trouble Victor Smith had made for himself by doing a similar thing on a bus with just a oncer. This memory, and what seemed to be Victor's urging, made me turn my back on the man to ease a fiver from the wallet.

Then I heard his gentle voice from behind me.

'I can guess what you're up to, you know. There's no need to go to that sort of extreme, Mavis. We're old friends. Yesterday was the tenth anniversary of our first meeting. Don't you remember? I thought that was why you'd come to see me today.'

'Yes,' I lied. 'It was.'

I turned to face him, holding the big white banknote before me. I felt foolish and tried to smile.

His eyebrows shot up in comical fashion.

'How about seeing what you can do with this?' I said, handing the banknote over.

'Where on Earth did you get so much money, Mavis?'

I thought quickly.

'Don't ask me,' I said. 'Ask Victor.'

'Victor Smith.' He almost spat the name out. 'Well, he deserved all you gave him after what he did to us. Others, too, I shouldn't wonder. Let's try to forget him for a while and have something to eat. Sorry, I've only got beans on toast to offer you until tomorrow.'

He looked at the damp bag on the floor.

'But first, I must go outside to burn all this stuff. Then I'll call around the second-hand shop and see what I can find for you. You just sit down there and take it easy. And, for goodness' sake, don't answer the door if anyone knocks. It may just be the police.'

With distaste, he picked up the bag containing the bloodstained clothes, donned his own woollen hat and scarf, and left through the front door.

Who was Charlie? Why was he being so helpful? Most of all, how could he take being the near-witness – or perhaps even witness – to a bloody murder with such equanimity? It did seem from what he'd said that Mavis had known him since around 1950. He also clearly knew and despised Victor Smith, but still…

*

'Mavis?'

He was bending over me. While he was out I must have fallen asleep. I looked at him properly for the first time. His face was smooth and he had a full head of white hair, despite his obvious age. His expression was kindly and there was concern, and perhaps something more, in his rheumy blue eyes.

'Why are you doing all this for me, Charlie?'

'Why am I doing all this? Well, wouldn't you expect me to, after-'

He didn't get the chance to finish his explanation. At that moment a sharp rap came a the door.

'Quick!' he hissed. 'Back upstairs. Hide yourself. Go in the bedroom this time. It's bigger. Keep quiet, no matter what. Take this bag of clothes I've just bought for you. It's sure to be the police. Someone has found Victor's body. I knew it wouldn't take long.'

It was indeed the police. A gruff voice announced the fact soon after we heard the knock. I hurried up the wooden staircase, trying to be quiet about doing so.

There were only two rooms, besides the landing, on the upper floor of this tiny house. These were the bathroom I'd already been in to dress myself in Charlie's nightgear and one bedroom. The latter was large, but its furnishings and décor made those of Jim Corcoran in Cypress Close, North Ruislip, look positively luxurious.

I dived into the bedroom as a second, less patient, knock came at the door and crouched down behind the unmade bed, next to a rickety table, and strained my ears to listen.

Downstairs, Charlie waited until they'd knocked twice more before I heard him opening the door. I hoped he hadn't kept the police waiting for too long.

Above my inadequate hiding place, on top of the table was a framed photograph, showing Charlie, beaming between two female figures. His arms were draped around the shoulders of both. With a start I realised that I – well, Mavis, at least – was the younger of the two women in the picture.

I didn't have too much time to ponder what I'd seen. From where I was I could hear the tones of one of the policemen, loud but muffled. I could hear the quieter, higher-pitched voice of Charlie well enough, though.

'I told you, officer. I was upstairs, just starting to make the bed when you knocked. I came down as quickly as I could. When you get to my age, you're not as quick on your pins as you were.'

More muffled tones. Then a clearer voice carried upstairs to me. This must have been that of the second policeman, who was speaking for the first time.

'I thought I heard some footsteps on the stairs before Charlie opened the door to us, George. It does sound as if he must be telling us what happened. Not that I'd ever say you'd tell us an untruth, you understand, Charlie.'

The second voice sounded younger, kinder. The deep, hectoring tones of George started again and went on at length. Charlie answered quietly to whatever he was saying, mainly by saying little more than 'yes' or 'no'. The younger policeman remained silent.

At last, the conversation sounded like it was coming to an end. I could only make out one more sentence of it, this time spoken by the younger policeman.

'Don't forget what the sergeant and I said, Charlie. This looks like the work of a maniac. Whoever he is, he may still be on the prowl. If you see or hear anything suspicious, let us know right away. We'll be back tomorrow, just to make sure everything's all right with you. Tonight, you make sure to lock your door!'

Soon after, that, I heard the door closing.

He! The police were assuming a man had killed Victor Smith.

'Mavis!' called Charlie ten or so minutes later. 'I think it's safe for you to come down now.'

Hesitantly, I descended. Charlie was almost beaming at me. Not long before, he'd seen me murder someone, or had at least seen the immediate aftermath. What was going on?

'I think I'd better be on my way.'

'Don't be foolish, girl. The police might not be be looking for you, but it wouldn't be wise for you to be seen wandering around here at this time. Still, you'd better leave in the morning. They'll be coming back tomorrow.' He sighed. 'To think, all these years I've been trying to get you to stay here with me and now I'm telling you to be on your way tomorrow.'

So that was it. Old Charlie needed a woman. His standards weren't very high, if Mavis fitted the bill.

'What do you want from me, Charlie?' I couldn't help blurting this out.

'What do I want? Well, I want you to have a look at those clothes I managed to find for you, for a start. Bet you haven't even looked inside the bag yet, have you? Then, like I said, I want to cook us both some beans on toast. I'm starving, even if you're not.'

He smiled engagingly. How could I ask him the questions I really wanted to have answered? An image floated into my mind.

'That photograph you have in the bedroom upstairs…'

'Ah, yes. That was taken in 1952 in Battersea Park, the summer after the Festival of Britain. The year before Babs…'

Charlie fumbled for his handkerchief and blew hard into it.

'Charlie,' I said. 'I didn't mean to…' Didn't mean to do what, exactly? But the old man was so visibly upset.

'No, no, everything's fine, Mavis. It's just when I think of that time…'

'Please don't upset yourself, Charlie.'

'No, I realise now you haven't seen that photograph before. Babs was your friend, just as she was my... my wife. But surely you remember the picture being taken? It was when the three of us were standing by the Fountain Lake.'

I, Stephen Charles, had never even been to the Pleasure Gardens, nor to any other site of the Festival of Britain. I barely remembered the Festival itself. The visit we were going to make from the children's home was cancelled at short notice.

'Yes,' I lied, smiling. 'I remember.' What else could I say? Where had almost every one of Mavis's memories gone? This Ka business did such unpredictable things with the mind and personality.

'Now, I'd better get on with doing those beans.'

*

Over our frugal meal and two leisurely cups of tea. I struggled to piece more of the story together.

'Where was it I met Babs, now? I can't remember at the moment.'

Charlie looked puzzled and not a little hurt.

'Surely you must remember a thing like that, Mavis? You and Babs were always talking about your first meeting. The day after New Year, it was. Babs was crossing that patch of waste ground behind the house when her shopping bag broke. Absolutely everywhere, all the stuff went. You were coming the other way and helped her to pick it up.'

'Ah, yes. I recall the day. It had slipped my mind for a moment.'

I should be more careful. Charlie was looking at me peculiarly.

'Are you sure everything is well, my girl? I mean, meeting the likes of Victor Smith like that would be hard for any woman, let alone you.'

'Yes I'm OK, thanks. It was when I first met you that I was really thinking about.'

'Well, that was only a few weeks later. Babs ran into you a second time, in more or less the same spot. She insisted on bringing you home to meet me.' He laughed to himself. 'You wouldn't come in at first. You thought a lady of the road wouldn't be good enough for me. Well, you certainly were good enough. Whenever you were in the area, we'd go off somewhere together, just the three of us.'

I tried to smile at these happy memories I didn't have. But Charlie was looking wistful.

'What's wrong, Charlie?'

'You know what I was thinking, Mavis. We thought those days would last for ever. But no, not much more than three years after we met they were no more. Just a week after the new Queen's coronation. In June it was. Oh, my Babs! Damn that Victor Smith!'

Babs had died; I'd already gleaned that much. Now it seened certain that she'd been killed. Looking at Charlie's expression, I could see that he was utterly convinced Victor Smith was responsible. I didn't have the heart to ask any more about what had happened. After all, Mavis was supposed to know.

'You know, I only wish I could do something.' I didn't know what else to say.

'But you already have done more than anyone, Mavis! That's why I've tried to get you to stay here with me. Tonight is the first night we'll be sleeping under the same roof together. Mavis, that means a lot to me.'

We talked for another half-hour. Despite my gentle probing, I could get no more out of him on the story of a past I had never shared, even if the old Mavis had shared some of it. All the time I was getting more and more tired. And all the time I was deeply conscious that there was only one bed upstairs…

After my fifth yawn, Charlie smiled at me.

'Now, come on, Mavis. It's high time you turned in. I'm more than a bit worn out myself, to tell you the truth. You can have a look at those clothes in the morning.'

'No, it's all right. I'm…' I was too tired to finish the sentence.

Charlie's warm smile became a gentle laugh.

'You're more than ready for that nice big bed upstairs, I'd say, my girl.'

'I'll sleep in your chair. It's bigger than this one. That'll be fine for me.'

I said this too quickly.

'Oh no you won't. Not with a comfy bed upstairs.'

'Charlie… I…' What was I going to say? That I wasn't Mavis? That I was really Steve Charles? That I'd occupied other bodies, including the one of his hated enemy, Victor Smith?

'Anyway, I'll be needing this chair for myself tonight. You can't sleep in the one you're in now, you know. It would never do for the two of us to be sleeping in the same room. Babs would never forgive us if we did that. No, you get yourself upstairs. No more talking for tonight.'

I could have kissed him.

*

'You sure you've got everything you need this morning?'

'Everything. Thanks again for this little suitcase. But tell me, Charlie, why are you doing all this for me?'

'You know why I'm doing what you're calling *all this* for you. Besides, this will be the last chance that comes my way.'

'Don't say last chance. There'll be another time when –'

Charlie smiled sadly.

'Enough now, Mavis. We won't talk about it. There's an old Anglo-Saxon expression: *Lyf is leone*. It means 'life is a loan'. Every one of us has a limited time on this Earth. Now it's time for you to be on your way.'

Anglo-Saxon? How did Charlie know a thing like that? He looked somehow resigned to his end as he said it. But was my own time on Earth limited? It didn't look that way.

*

I did have everything I needed. Not only this small suitcase, the clothes Charlie had bought for me from somewhere, and the rest of the money – I still had all those fivers – but last night I had found something tucked into Mavis's worn brassiere. It was to prove to be more valuable than any of them.

The card was safely in the pocket of the smart woman's jacket I now wore. This morning I woke in the belief, perhaps built on no sure foundation, that somehow this small piece of cardboard was going to change my whole life. I felt its sharp corners now and could picture it in my mind.

It was marked on the front only with a typed name and address on one side: '*Sister Gloria, Sunshine Mission, Landford Road, Putney*'. But it was the reverse that really intrigued me. There was a handwritten pencil note in tiny script: '*Mavis – please, please come and see me again. You have a God-given talent and I'm sure it could benefit not only those in our*

Mission but also many of the unfortunates in our nation. Sister Gloria.'

That was all it said. What did it mean? From the look of the smudged pencil and creases in the card, Mavis had been carrying it for some time, trying to decide whether or not to take up the invitation.

Well, I wouldn't wait a moment longer to find out what very real talent I was supposed to possess. I'd get myself down to Landford Road just as soon as I could. But first of all, I'd better get my hair tidied up. The clothes I wore were more or less presentable, but my hair was a tangled mess.

I walked for quite some way, finding myself on the fringes of Putney before I located what I was looking for, a not-too-smart hairdressing salon with a prominent sign to say that appointments were not always necessary. There were no other customers in the shop and I should have thought appointments with the single hairdresser would rarely have been necessary.

*

'Well, there we are then,' Sheila was saying. 'I thought you'd wanted it cut too short, but I have to say it does look smart. A shampoo with this and you'll be all set. The charge for both will be two guineas. I hope you've got the right change. Not much in the shop today, I'm afraid.'

Two guineas! Sheila certainly knew how to charge. But change was the one thing I didn't have. I had only fivers and was reluctant to produce one of those. Sheila would be unlikely to be able to find the change for this. I thought quickly.

'Can you do me a facial?'

'Not something I specialise in, I'm afraid.'

'I'll give you three quid if you do whatever you can. Just a bit of eyeliner, cream and lipstick. Nothing too tarty. You see, I only have a fiver.'

Sheila couldn't have looked more pained if I'd hit her in the stomach.

'Only a fiver?' she said, incredulously. 'But there's not two quid in the shop to give you in change. You're my first customer of the day.'

'*And probably the last,*' I thought, unkindly. But to Sheila, I said, 'You do what you can and give me whatever change you have in the shop.'

She looked at me dubiously.

'I could tint your hair for you. A nice blonde or redhead? I've got a lovely shade – a kind of dark orange it is, really. Or maybe brunette would suit you? You've still got a few nice streaks of brown in all that grey. I could do what I could to match your natural colour.'

Hair dye? I wanted Mavis to look respectable for Sister Gloria, not to present herself like some faded film star. I didn't think that a flame-haired tart would go down well at the Sunshine Mission.

'No thanks,' I said hastily. 'Just my face. And don't overdo the eyeshadow. Keep it light'

I wanted to add, '*Much lighter than yours, Sheila. You look exactly like an out-of-work whore.*' To express this thought – I had no idea where it came from – would have hardly been diplomatic so, instead, I smiled as winningly as I could. As I did this, I looked at my reflection in Sheila's mirror. With short hair, Mavis already looked much smarter than I'd have thought possible. I realised I must have overestimated her age by at least ten years.

'Well,' she said. 'If you're sure. I'll have to go in the back room afterwards to get some stuff. I'll need to see what change I can rustle up while I'm at it. Let's do the rinse.'

When Sheila had finished the shampoo and disappeared into her back room – this was more of a large cupboard, in truth – I surreptitiously eased a fiver from Father Grey's wallet. There was no real reason why a respectable woman like the one now beginning to emerge from within the vagrant Mavis shouldn't be using a wallet, even one laden with wealth, but it still felt more than a shade illegal.

'Right, let's see what we can do,' said Sheila, as she returned. 'We'll have all the men running after you soon. They seem to like this mature businesswoman look these days and I must say we have some promising material here.'

I sighed. It was clear that I'd have to work hard to slow down Sheila's enthusiasm with the powder and paint.

*

She'd only been able to produce a pound and four shillings in change for my fiver. At three pounds sixteen shillings, this must have been the most expensive trim, rinse and application of lipstick ever, especially when I'd had to do so much direction when it came to the latter.

Still, the eventual result was more or less what I wanted and at least I could walk into the café a few doors down from the hairdresser's and had some sensible money to buy sausage and chips, with a cup of tea.

Afterwards, it took me the best part of two hours to find Landford Road in Putney, the home of the Sunshine Mission. There was no sign of anyone in a nun's habit, only a few men and women with blank faces and two women in earnest conversation near the doorway.

These two clearly had some official presence, so I waited for them to finish. When they did, the older of the two flashed her dazzlingly gleaming spectacles in my direction, smiled brightly at me, and marched over to where I stood.

'Welcome!' she said. 'We weren't expecting anyone, but I'm oh-so pleased to see you. The hordes will all be in during the next half-hour for their sausage roll and cuppa, and there's only Linda and me on duty today. We're short handed again. You have come to volunteer, I hope?'

I stared at her, blankly.

'No; not exactly,' I said. 'I've come in to see Sister Gloria.'

The woman looked indignant.

'Well, really!' she said. 'The Sister promised not to do this sort of thing again. She promised to leave all the administration to me.' Her cross expression softened.

'Look, I'm sorry. This is hardly your fault. The Sister only looks in three times a week. She should be in soon to help with our visitors – if she's on time, that is. I'm Mrs Weatherall, by the way.'

'I'm Mavis.'

Mrs Weatherall looked at me quizzically.

'Mavis what?'

Mavis what, indeed? I had no clue.

'Mavis Charles,' I answered, giving her my own, Steve Charles's surname, and wishing I'd had the sense to invent one for Mavis.

'Well, Mrs Charles, perhaps you'd like to take a seat in Sister Gloria's office? She'll be with you just as soon as we've dealt with the initial onslaught of the ravening multitudes.'

I was shown into Sister Gloria's office by Mrs Weatherall, who closed the door behind me without a word. This 'office' was a small, bare affair. It was furnished only with a small table. By no stretch of imagination could this be called a desk, with nothing but a spindly chair on each side of it.

On the wall was a single, stark crucifix of indeterminate age. This was hardly much to keep me occupied, so all I could do was listen to the gentle build-up of sound coming through the door.

The noise must be that made by what Mrs Weatherall had called, in an unflattering way, 'the ravening multitudes'. It seemed as if she and Linda were going to have their hands full, even if Mrs Weatherall's simile for them seemed extreme.

After I had been waiting for fifteen minutes and the sound of the people outside had risen to a steady hum, I heard the telephone on the wall outside ringing.

'Yes?' It was Mrs Weatherall's distinctive voice. I could hear her high-pitched tones quite clearly.

There followed a period when she said nothing beyond a series of 'I sees' in increasing volume. The party at the other end of the line must have been delivering unwelcome news.

'Well, this is very awkward... Oh, I see... It's as bad as that is it? Yes, I'll tell her... No, I'll just have to cope as best I can. Bye.'

I heard the sound of the phone being replaced and the whispered tones of a hurried conversation between Mrs Weatherall and the silent person outside I'd assumed to be Linda – she hadn't been introduced in any way. Minutes later, a gentle knock came at the door of Sister Gloria's office. It was opened by Mrs Weatherall, who entered with a timidity that surprised me.

'Mrs Charles. I'm so sorry to disturb you. Look, I'll have to come straight to the point. Linda's aunt has become unwell and I've had to send her home. This couldn't have happened at a worse time. The people are already starting to come in, demanding their sausage rolls, and Sister Gloria hasn't turned up yet. There should be three of us, and I find myself on my own.'

'Is there anything I can do?'

'Oh, *would* you, Mrs Charles? It's really highly irregular of me to even think of asking. The formalities of your volunteering haven't been completed but... Oh, but I am so truly desperate, Mrs Charles.'

Formalities... desperate... Such language! She only wanted help with serving a few sausage rolls, for goodness' sake. If I told her my name and history , she'd surely have had a heart attack. If I also told her Mavis's name probably wasn't really 'Mrs Charles', and I had not the faintest clue as to what it might have been, she'd have a double heart attack..

'Don't worry about it, Mrs Weatherall,' I said. 'Just tell me what you want me to do.'

'Beryl, please. Call me Beryl. Well, if you wouldn't mind buttering the rolls and slipping the sausages inside them... Perhaps you'd also be able to manage the washing-up; we haven't enough plates and cups for everyone all at once. I'll serve the people and pour the tea. Come on... Mavis. We'd better get out there before they start stamping their feet or whatever these people do when they become impatient.'

Well, at least 'Mavis' was an improvement on 'Mrs Charles'.

*

We coped easily. They weren't even proper sausage rolls we were serving; just sausages wrapped in a slice of buttered bread. I had to give Mrs Weatherall – Beryl – a hand with pouring the tea, and I was always scurrying between the tiny sink in the kitchen behind and the trestle table from which we served, but there was nothing particularly hard about what we did. Beryl didn't think so, though.

'Phew! Thank goodness that's done,' she said. 'Next week, I'm going to insist there are three of us here for this job, without fail. I hope Linda will be back with us by then. I'm going to tell Sister Gloria that if she can't make it herself, she'll simply have to send someone else from the convent. Or perhaps you might be with us properly by next week, Mavis?'

At that moment, a woman in nun's habit entered the mission building. She looked supremely calm. I guessed this to be Sister Gloria.

'Good afternoon, Mrs Weatherall. I'm so sorry I'm late. Last minute convent business, you understand. I see you have a member of the public with you.' She favoured me with a warm smile. 'Linda couldn't make it this week, then?'

Beryl's expression was stony.

'This is Mrs Charles, Sister. She's come to see you – as you should very well know. But before you speak to Mrs Charles, I'd like a word with you myself, if I may. An urgent word.'

Sister Gloria looked perplexed.

'No, I don't know Mrs Charles.' She looked at me again. 'You do look oddly familiar, though, Mrs Charles. Have we met before somewhere?'

'No, we haven't – not really.'

This was a vague answer. But I could hardly tell her the truth. And I knew nothing about the previous meeting Mavis and the Sister must surely have had for Sister her to have written what she did.

'Sister Gloria...' Beryl was looking impatient.

'I haven't forgotten we need to speak, Mrs Weatherall.' There was some confusion in the Sister's eyes as she turned her face towards me. 'Would you mind waiting in my office for a few minutes, Mrs Charles? It's just-'

'I know where it is,' I said.

*

Back in Sister Gloria's office, I decided to close the door and sat in one of the only two chairs. It would be rude to eavesdrop. Besides, I could imagine what was being said. Beryl would be nagging Sister Gloria for more help. This was a thing I thought she hardly needed.

In the austere room, I wondered whether Beryl would express the hope that I would join Linda and her in the weekly tea-and-sausage-roll ceremony.

I'd been expecting, probably on no firm foundation, a lot more from Sister Gloria's pencilled note. I could see this in my mind's eye: '*Mavis – please come and see me again. You have a real talent and I'm sure it could benefit not only our Mission but also many of the unfortunates in our nation. Sister Gloria.'*

Many more than a few minutes had passed before the Sister opened the door, carrying a sheet of paper in her hand. Once again, there was the same look on her face. She regarded me with an expression I'd have to describe as halfway between confusion and recognition.

'I'm so sorry to have kept you waiting, Mrs Charles. I'll come straight to the point. The truth is that we're puzzled about you. No-one but Beryl or me would have asked you to come along today. We're quite sure neither of us did. I even telephoned the convent to see if someone there has their wires crossed, but they couldn't help me.

'Of course, if you wanted to volunteer you'd be more than welcome. Mrs Weatherall would welcome it especially. All I'd need from you are a few details for this form. Mrs Weatherall insists on the form, even if you've already filled one one in somewhere along the way. It will have been lost along the way, I'm afraid.'

She waved her sheet of paper and smiled. Then she gave me another of her penetrating looks.

'You know, Mrs Charles, I'm beginning to feel sure we must have met before. In this very room, I believe. Yet it can't be. I have a good memory and I've only been a member of the mission for eighteen months... Have you ever been here for any other reason than to volunteer?'

I decided to put her out of her misery and took out the card she'd written at some time in the past.

'Mavis? Don't you remember meeting me? The woman with talent, you said?'

I handed her the card. As much as anything else, I was curious as to what talent this might be.

Her eyes widened and lit up.

'Well, of course I do, now! Mavis! Such a wonderful woman, I thought at the time, if more than a little lost, I had to fear. It was the best part of a year ago I wrote this card – and it was indeed in this very room. But somehow you look so very different today. I should have realised straight away. You look as if you could be a younger cousin, or one could almost say daughter of the woman I spoke to then.'

'I am Mavis Charles,' I said. The words felt odd on my lips. I wanted to tell the Sister I was really *Steve* Charles. But at least I had a proper surname again, and it was my own, even if I was the wrong sex.

'But you look so much different from the way you were when last I saw you. More...'

'More human?' I said. 'It's surprising what a bath, new clothes and a visit to a hairdresser can do.'

I didn't add anything about the banknotes in the priest's wallet.

'No, I wouldn't say a thing like that,' she said.

She'd have thought it, though.

'But it's so wonderful to see you again, Mavis. Tell me, what brought you back? I didn't expect to see you here again, after what you said when we met before.'

What had Mavis said to Sister Gloria last time? I had no clue. How could I answer? I decided to tell her the truth.

'It was your note, Sister Gloria. The note you put on the back of that card. I thought about it afterwards.'

'My note? You mean you'll do what we talked about? Oh, Mavis, I'm overjoyed.'

What was it we'd talked about? What was it I'd said I'd do? I couldn't imagine Sister Gloria would want the old Mavis to be serving tea and sausage rolls in the Sunshine Mission. Beryl Weatherall certainly wouldn't. Besides, that hardly needed much in the way of talent

'Yes,' I said. 'Of course I'll do it'. What other answer could I give, even though I still had no clue as to what 'it' was?

'I'm so pleased! You have a natural talent and I'm glad it will be used for good. Tell you what, I don't have to leave for the convent for another half hour. Shall we give it a little run-through now? Not a proper one of course. We can do it more seriously tomorrow.'

'If you like.'

A run-through? What on Earth had I – what had Mavis – agreed to do?

Sister Gloria shuffled the papers in her bag. She pulled out a single sheet of paper and handed it to me.

'There. It's nothing much, I'm afraid. Not really suitable for what we want. It will do for the moment, though. It's just the draft of a press release I'm putting together. The convent will be opening a new playgroup for the little ones in Putney next month.'

'What am I supposed to do with this?

She looked at me blankly.

'Why, read it out loud, of course. It doesn't matter what it's about. Just stand over there in the middle of the room and read it out in your wonderful way. Pretend you're on a stage facing a crowd of people. Read it – perform it – with the kind of emphasis I know you can give so well.'

Now, even in those days, I was far from illiterate. I could certainly read well enough but I hated to do this out loud. In school I'd always stumbled my way through any reading-aloud task and now, frankly, the prospect terrified me.

I used to play truant whenever I could anticipate the teacher's command coming my way. Now, six years later, I knew that terror once again. In fact, over those six years it had become more intense.

'I-I-'

'Go on, Mavis. Just as you did last time.'

I walked unsteadily to my feet towards the centre of the small room. It was hardly more than two yards to reach the centre of the Sister

Gloria's office, but it felt all of two miles. I faced Sister Gloria – one person was one too many – and gulped noisily.

'On Monday, the five – fifteen – fifteenth of Febru-ru-rry, the Sunny Mission will… I can't do this, Sister… I just can't do it.'

Sister Gloria regarded me with surprise and concern.

'Mavis, what's wrong today? You spoke beautifully not as much as a year ago.'

I thought quickly.

'I've had a trauma.'

This excuse sounded familiar to me, although I couldn't think why.

'What sort of trauma?'

Sister Gloria looked puzzled.

'I don't want to talk about it yet, if you don't mind.'

Nor could I speak about it until I'd invented a story. But I was tired of inventing stories.

'Well…,' said Sister Gloria. 'If I don't know what the problem is, I don't see that I can help. Let's see … I suggest you go home, or to wherever you're sleeping at the moment and have a good rest. I'll be here again in the morning. We can give it another try and perhaps you'll be able to tell me more then.'

Sister Gloria smiled in a confused way and made as if to rise. I remained standing.

What was I going to do? I had no idea how a vagrant woman in London should survive, and I could hardly go back to Charlie's house so soon.

I hadn't exactly coped at all well as a vagrant man. I started to think of putting some of the funds I still had in Father Grey's wallet to use – a rooming house, perhaps. But what issued from my lips was pure panic.

'Sister, I have nowhere to go. Absolutely nowhere. What can I do?'

For a long moment, the nun simply looked at me, dumbfounded.

'Mavis, I don't understand. You were always such a resourceful woman, in your special way.' Her features softened. 'As you know, we can't provide accommodation as part of our work but, as it happens, we do have one small room at the back I can let you use.

'It will have to be only for two nights at most, I'm afraid. Then we'll have to point you in some other direction. Unless…'

Then she smiled. An unforced, broad smile, it was.

'I'll go and have a word with Mrs Weatherall. Wait here.'

She rose from her seat and left the room. The door closed with a loud click. Fifteen minutes later, the door was partially opened by Beryl Weatherall. She poked her head through.

'Are you all right, Mavis, love?' she said. 'Sister Gloria has asked me to show you to the room at the back. I can find you somewhere better for only thirty shillings if you like. Bit of domestic trouble, is it? Never mind, that can happen to any one of us. Of course, I'd put you up myself if I could. But you know how it is.'

So, Beryl still looked upon me as someone like herself, although with some temporary marital difficulty, did she? I was a very long way from being in that position.

What had Sister Gloria had said to her? The offer of *somewhere better* did sound wildly tempting and I certainly had the money to pay for a room for a short time. But where would I be afterwards? Charlie was an old man, after all, and it would be unfair to think of burdening him in the longer term.

I just might need every penny of the money in the wallet sooner rather than later.

'No,' I said. 'The room upstairs will be perfect for a night or two.'

'Two nights will be all you can have it for, I'm afraid. It is very small. But Sister Gloria did say she felt sure the two of you would be able to work out the little problem you had with using your gift tomorrow morning and everything would be fine then. She didn't have time to tell me what that problem was, nor your gift. You can tell me yourself when you're ready. You know I won't pry.'

She smiled encouragingly at me, clearly hoping I was going to tell her something now. Little problem? For me to speak in public would be impossible.

'I'm really tired, Beryl. I need to rest.'

*

The problem facing me may not have been a little one, as Sister Gloria had breezily dismissed it, but 'the room at the back' was indeed *tiny*. Beryl Weatherall and I could hardly both stand in it together. Besides the tired-looking camp bed, the only furnishings were a crooked wooden chair, a crucifix on one wall and, just above it, a small shelf, home to a few forlorn books that looked as if they hadn't been touched for years.

I don't know how long I sat on that chair thinking about my future. What future? Then my eye happened to fall upon the title of one of the neglected books: *The Deeper Meaning of Psalm 23*. Deeper meaning? I didn't know this one even had a deep meaning to begin with.

If it hadn't been for something about the attractive gold lettering on the dusty dark crimson title spine, my attention might have wandered off elsewhere. Probably I'd soon have been asleep.

As it was, despite my tiredness, I found myself going over to fetch the book. Soon I was reading. It was extraordinary. Unlike my inability to read aloud, I'd never been a slouch at reading to myself. But I found myself reading extraordinarily quickly.

It was as if my hands turning the pages and my eyes scanning the words on them had become nothing more than physical intermediaries to enable the ideas the book contained to flow deep into the core of my being. Sounds pretentious, doesn't it? But this is the way it was. After the first few minutes it wasn't like normal reading at all.

But I tell you, as I flipped over page after page, I was really understanding, at least at the time, what those ideas were. Chapter two, for instance, made much of what it called the standard translation of verse five, which it gave as: *'You prepare a table before me in the presence of my enemies; You anoint my head with oil; my cup overflows.'*

The book claimed that this translation was imprecise and had lost the intended meaning, as a careful reading of the Hebrew original would reveal. It argued that, while the word *Neged* can often indeed mean simply 'in the presence of in the case of this, the best-known of all Psalms, it has a more confrontational stance, as in 'against' [my enemies].

This and hundreds of similar ideas, far too subtle for me to grasp now, or even to remember in most cases, were crystal clear to me on that January afternoon in the Sunshine Mission. It was still not yet quite dark by the time I finished the book. And then I fell asleep.

*

'Mavis?'

Where was I? Who was I? These were the first thoughts I had next morning.

Blinking, and only slowly coming to, I began to realise that I was in a borrowed bed in the tiny back bedroom of somewhere called the Sunshine Mission. What was I doing here? And who was the black-clad woman leaning over me and beaming down at me?

'Good morning... Sister Gloria.' At the last moment, even as I spoke, her name came back to me.

'I'm so glad you slept so well,' she said. 'I've been in for half an hour. You were sleeping so deeply when I looked in that I didn't like to disturb you. But I have to be away by eleven. We'll just have time to put right the little problem we had yesterday.'

Sister Gloria beamed down upon me again.

'After a little breakfast for you of course. It's only tea and biscuits, I'm afraid. That's all we have. Besides leftover sausage rolls from yesterday. You wouldn't want one of those *ghastly* things. Stay there, Mavis. I'll see to it and bring something in to you myself.'

With that, she swept out of the room. Actually, I'd have liked nothing better than a sausage roll at that moment. But a darker thought soon came to dominate my thoughts. What Sister Gloria had jauntily called 'the little problem we had yesterday' was an impassable barrier as far I was concerned.

*

'Whenever you're ready to start reading, Mavis.'

I gulped, for some reason tasting the over-seasoned sausage rolls from yesterday I hadn't even eaten, rather than the two dry biscuits I'd just breakfasted on.

'Go on, please, Mavis.'

I looked down at the same draft press release as Sister Gloria had given me to read yesterday. The words started to blur in my vision. Closing my eyes, I wanted the Earth to swallow me up.

Then, quite suddenly, the red-blackness starting to form in my vision shimmered before me. It was to be replaced by the clear vision of attractive gold lettering on the crimson title spine of a book. I seemed to hear a voice from somewhere within. '*Relax. You leave it to me,*' the voice seemed to be saying.

I opened my eyes and spoke: '*Miz mohr leh David, ahdohnoi rohee loh ekh sar*'.

Sister Gloria's mouth dropped open. Somehow, although I couldn't understand any of the words I was saying, apart from 'David', I knew I was quoting the opening of Psalm 23 from the original Hebrew.

Then I launched into a clear explanation of some of the points in Pslam. I gave a short history of David writing while he was on the run from King Saul. Some of these ideas were touched on in the book I read last night. From where some of the others came I had no idea.

Sister Gloria, always so self-possessed before now, could only look on in amazement.

After some even more complicated points about why the standard translation of Psalm 23 should be treated with caution, I launched into a few anecdotes about life on the road and what they should mean to those more fortunate in this life.

This I could relate to, even though I had only briefly shared such a life with both Victor and Mavis... Mavis... It was clearly her and not me, Steve Charles, speaking. Was I truly Steve Charles any longer?

Sister Gloria held up her hand.

'Enough, Mavis. You're even more eloquent than you were when I saw you last year. And the things you know! I can arrange a small audience for you as early as tomorrow.

After that - let's see what I can do. You must
rest and take it easy before then.'

'But-,' I started to say.'

'Don't worry, Mavis. I know you have a
temporary accommodation difficulty. I can help
with that. And I don't mean you can use that
poky back room here at the mission. You're
coming home with me.'

*

Sister Gloria was as good as her word. She
had a pleasant house tucked away in a genteel
part of Putney. I had the smaller of the two
bedrooms, but it was a comfortable one. It was
the first good bedroom I'd had in my life. Or
should I say that it was the first good bedroom
Steve Charles had enjoyed in his life. Or was I
even right to still think of myself as Steve
Charles? By this time, I honestly wasn't sure
who I was.

*

Two days after moving into Sister Gloria's
house, I made my first public speaking
appearance. It was more stuff about the Psalms
of David, but it went amazingly well, every bit
as well as Sister Gloria had hoped. Even better.
As for me, I was nervous at first, but found that

if I relaxed and let Mavis take over, as it were, it all came very easily.

I made two more appearances within a week. After the second was the time Bryony came into my life. After my performance – that is the right word – she, still a very young woman at the time, walked up to me with a smile on her face.

'Mavis? May I call you that? Bryony Richards I am'.

Why not? Mavis was as accurate as many other names she could have used.

'I have to get back to Putney soon, though. I have another talk to give tomorrow evening and Sister Gloria has arranged something else for me in the morning.'

'More churchie stuff?' Bryony smiled. 'I can put you on the path to so much more.'

Something about the way she said it, or perhaps just her gently mocking smile, threw me. Mavis was dormant at this time and the only sacramental memories Steve Charles possessed were barely remembered ones from early childhood, when he stood beside the mother he could never quite picture in St Mary's Church in North Ruislip.

'Well … it's what I know about.'

This was hardly true. Since those almost forgotten days, Steve Charles had even tried to avoid walking past any church.

At that moment, Sister Gloria popped her head around the doorway to the hall.

'Just about ready, Mavis? We have to be at St Hugh's by ten o'clock tomorrow morning.'

If Sister Gloria hadn't added that bit about St Hugh's, I may have gone with her. As it was, I could see a lifetime of draughty church halls and earnest discussion groups ahead of me. Sister Gloria hadn't even told me why we were going to St Hugh's. That was the point at which I rebelled.

'I have a slight headache, Sister Gloria. A walk in the fresh air is the thing for me. If I walk down to near the river, I can catch a bus all the way back to Putney. And I can use that front door key you were good enough to have cut for me this morning. I'll be home well before nine o'clock this evening.'

'It'll be dark by then. It's already beginning to get dark now.'

'Come on, Sister Gloria. You know I've been out in the dark before.' I couldn't entirely suppress a chuckle as I spoke.

'If you're sure…' said Sister Gloria.

Anyone could see, as she quietly closed the double oak doors, that Sister Gloria was anything but sure herself. Nor should she have been. The key, unused, was thrown into the Thames one week later. I never saw Sister Gloria again. I often regret that I didn't give a freebie talk or two for her after that night. But the plain fact is that I didn't.

At the home of young Bryony Richards that evening, I had a small glass of rum with honey rather than a large mug of sweet cocoa. Steve Charles had never been a particular fan of spirits, but I'd discovered over the last week or so that I absolutely detested cocoa.

'Well,' said Bryony, as we sipped our nightcaps, 'I'm your business manager now. What's it going to be?'

'I'm sorry?'

'You can hardly talk about the Gospels, the Psalms, or that sort of thing, can you? Not if you hope to draw paying audiences, at least.' Bryony laughed. 'No money in that for us. So,

what's it going to be? You've had an interesting
life. The choice is yours.'

I was dumbfounded. Mavis may indeed
have had a life that could be described as
'interesting' but I knew so little about it. The
only life I knew much about was that of Steve
Charles. Until November last year, that life had
been excessively dull.

And I knew next to nothing about the lives
of the unfortunate Jim Corcoran, who had been
wrongly hanged for 'my' murder, Hubert Grey,
the determined but unhealthy priest, or Victor
Smith, the unpleasant tramp. Even Mavis,
whose body I now inhabited and the one to
whom I already somehow felt closest, was a
mystery to me. I didn't even know her surname,
and had given her my own.

'Sorry to have taken you by surprise,' said
Bryony. 'A friend told me about you and
convinced me I should come see what you could
do on a platform. You don't suppose I usually
go into church halls to look for clients, do you?

'Anyway, before I even thought of coming
in here I did my homework. I've found out a bit
– I was unable to find out much at all – about
your life. I was surprised to learn you were a
lady of the road for years – what they're now

starting to call a bag lady. I thought you'd want to talk about that. You did tonight a little. You must have a lot to say on that subject.'

The next thing I said seemed to pop out of my mouth of its own accord.

'Yes, that's what I'll talk about. I'll talk about life on the road.'

In fact, my own memories of the tramping life were limited to brief periods in the lives of Victor Smith and Mavis Charles. I suppose I was hoping that Mavis would come to my rescue again.

*

This she did, and in a big way. You may even have read about me in the newspapers, under the stage name I assumed, naturally. But I was widely known as 'The Bag Lady' and soon became the recognised spokeswoman for those, men as well as women, who were forced to spend their lives on the road.

Less than a month after teaming up with Bryony. I made a determined effort to track Charlie down. He'd been so wonderfully helpful to me. I dread to think what might have happened otherwise.

Alas, I was to find Charlie had died not much more than a week after I'd left his house. So this was what he'd meant by his last chance? How tragic, when his last years must have been so empty for him, living alone. Yet Charlie had seemed so supremely content when I saw him, despite everything life had thrown at him.

*

My own life couldn't have been more different from that of Charlie. I was invited to sit on Government enquiries, church commissions and similar groups, whose members nodded earnestly, spoke at great length and, really, achieved very little.

What I – Mavis, in truth – was happiest doing, was telling anecdotes from a performance platform. I honestly think it brought more benefit to the homeless than all this committee business.

And over the years it made me, and Bryony, a lot of money. We both bought bigger, more luxurious houses.Both were in Ealing, as it happened. Bryony happily indulged her expensive obsession with cars. A few years later, although by then Mavis was not a young woman, I learned to drive myself and was surprised to discover I shared her passion. We played an unspoken, quietly competitive game between us, changing our cars regularly and showing them off to each other.

This was the luxuriously simple pattern of my life for the next twenty or so years: wealthy, well-known and well settled. Then on 3rd April, 1982, there came a ripple into this new life.

*

I can remember the date precisely. It was the day after the Falklands Islands had been siezed by a desperate Argentine dictator, anxious to prove to his people that he had what it takes to be a bold leader. But, to me, I remember it as the day on which I had a surprise visitor from the past. It was Steve Charles's past.

'Someone wants to see you,' announced Bryony, walking into my dressing room after a talk I'd given, not far from my home in Ealing. 'The man says he knows you well.'

'I'm tired, Bryony. Can't you make my excuses for me? It'll only be another gentleman of the road who'd have met me briefly somewhere. Maybe not even that. He's probably really only after a handout. Give him a tenner and send him on his way if you would.'

I usually made a point of seeing these unlucky people. Whether Mavis knew them or not I never had a clue, but the short time I had – Steve had – spent on the road was enough to make me want to listen to their sad stories for a few minutes before thrusting some money upon them. But on this day I did feel worn out and wanted to dispense with the listening part of it.

'I really do think you might want to see this man,' said Bryony. 'He told me he knew you from way back, during the war. I found out that you weren't on the road then. Remember we talked briefly about this?'

Yes, but where truly was I – Mavis – back before the war? I'd invented some brief details to shut Bryony up, but really, the past was a closed book. Some of these vagrant visitors would have known more about her life than Mavis did herself.

'I really don't want to speak to anyone from my past today.' What would be the point if I couldn't say whether I really knew him? 'I've seen too many visitors this week.'

For whatever reason, Bryony persisted.

'He really wants to talk to you, Mavis. I'm sure he's genuine. And this one isn't a-'

'Tramp?'

Bryony looked abashed.

'No. He looks quite respectable'.

'What's his name then?'

I knew by this time that, tired or not, I'd have to see him.

'Alan Milgram,'

'Go on, then.' I said. The name rang a small bell in my – in Steve's memory. With a shock, I realised that the young man's memory, in fact his whole consciousness, had been dormant for so long. 'I'll see him for just a moment.'

*

A few minutes later, in walked Al – Al from the card school and wallpaper factory in Parva-vale. His hair was pure white now and his expression was decidedly a worried one, not at all arrogant as before, but I recognised him straight away.

'Hello, Mavis. You look just the same as you did last time I saw you … must be all of forty years ago.'

So Al knew Mavis did he? I was taken aback to learn this. But I recovered enough to give him a bland response. I wanted to find out how he could know her from so long ago.

'Don't be silly, Al,' I said. 'We're all older now. A lot of water has passed under the bridge in forty years for us all.'

And, of most of those years, Mavis knew precisely nothing.

'More than water has passed under my bridge,' he said.

His tone told of a deep melancholy. This wasn't at all like the Al I knew from Steve Charles's days as factory worker. I felt I had to say something, however much I'd detested him then.

'We're all getting older, Al. Don't worry about it.'

'Mavis, he said. 'You're marvellous. No wonder I always carried a candle for you. From the day I first saw that photograph of you he always carried, it was. That was the cause of all the trouble, really. I was jealous. No two ways about it.

'But I know you never really liked me. Can't say I blame you. And now the docs are telling me I could go at any time. I've been carrying guilt around like a lead weight within me for more than forty years.'

Al's voice broke into something like a sob. I'd never before seen him like this.

'Twenty-odd years ago I made it all so much worse. I'm not asking for forgiveness from you or anyone else – I don't deserve that much. Just let me lighten the burden on my shoulders a little by telling you about these things while I still can. Then I'll be on my way. I won't trouble you again.'

There couldn't be any answer to what he was saying. I, Steve Charles, had detested Al. A fluttering feeling within me told me that Mavis felt the same about him. I merely nodded for him to continue. It was a full minute before Al could do so.

'At Jim's trial,' Al suddenly blurted out, 'I bore false witness against him.'

'I know all about that.'

As soon as I said those words, I realised Al could only have been talking about Jim Corcoran's trial. Al and I – or Jim, as far as the World was concerned – were there. But why should I – as Mavis – know which Jim he was talking about? Al didn't even seem to notice my slip. Why?

'You do? Well, I suppose you'd have had plenty of time to find out about everything. You always were like a little terrier with these things when we were younger.'

What on Earth was Al talking about?

'Everything I said in that court was a lie. I didn't even see Jim that night in Parva-vale, let alone speak to him. But the thing I did all those years before was even worse, somehow, even though what I said in that court – I can make no excuses for myself – would have made it easier for those legal vultures to convict Jim. But I knew I'd already ruined Jim's life. And…'

Here he lapsed into silence again. He was struggling to speak. I could make no sense of a single word he was saying.

'Go on.' This was all I could think of to say.

The silent moments that followed were the most unsettling thing. Al's words became even more laboured.

'I was always… the odd one out,' he managed to say. 'The other three never really accepted me –'

And that was it. Al slumped forward, dead. It really was that sudden.

After that, chaos. I'm sure I even passed out for a moment or two myself. I remember, or

think I remember, Bryony rushing in,
ambulance crews racing in soon after her, and
indulgent policemen talking to me concernedly.
Really, everything happened in a blur.

*

The episode upset me more than I thought
possible. I couldn't return to the platform for
two whole months. Bryony didn't want me to
go back to work even then. There was no need,
she said, we were both wealthy enough.

This was true. Thanks to my popularity
and her adept management, I could command
large fees. Apart from our indulgences with the
cars, we had spent and invested wisely. Neither
of us had any real material wants.

But still, *something* drove me on. I worked
a little less, though not much. Bryony herself
was getting older – she was in her fifties by that
time – and now worked exclusively on my
engagements.

She still had many other clients but all the
work for these was handled by Martyn Bedford,
her extraordinarily capable new assistant.
Bryony didn't allow young Martyn to do any of
my work except on the one occasion.

I'd been nagging Bryony again to help me
find out more about the earlier life of Mavis. As

the years passed, this was becoming something of an obsession with me. Eventually, and reluctantly, I thought, she put Martyn on the case.

To my knowledge, this was the only time he ever failed to come up with the goods. At the end of his work, I had the only longish conversation I ever experienced with him. He never spoke more than he needed to, Bryony told me.

Martyn visited me at home one day, a few months after Bryony had told me she'd given him the assignment. Sitting down in the chair opposite me, he was reluctant to say much at all, to start with. I could see before he uttered a word that he didn't have good news for me.

He was an alarmingly handsome and charming young man. Young was the right word, too. He was only somewhere in his twenties and I'm sure I – Mavis – wouldn't see sixty again but I began to have some insight of the way Bryony looked upon the young man.

Oh yes – it didn't need feminine insight to realise that Bryony was nursing a fading hope that they'd have a future together, even though her priority was to be highly competent and professional on the agency work she did for me.

'Mavis,' Martyn said at last. 'I don't know how to tell you this…'

'The straightforward way is usually best, Martyn. You haven't been able to find anything out about my earlier life, have you?'

He smiled gently.

'Mavis, I'm sorry. I haven't yet been able to find out anything worthwhile about your earlier life. Back in the ninteen-forties you lived somewhere in the outer suburbs, as far as I can find out, but of your friends, family and life at that time, I can tell you nothing.'

'Nothing?' I said. I thought I should at least not remain silent.

'Nothing,' Martyn echoed. 'Soon after the war, while still a fairly young woman, you turned up in Central London. You lived what they call "a life on the road". I suppose in your case it could have been called "a life on the river". The Thames, along much of its urban length, was where you had your "beat".'

I'd already worked out this much from what the unpleasant Victor Smith had said. But why had Mavis changed her life so drastically? Exactly what had happened in the outer suburbs this young man was talking about so breezily?

There was a little more to our conversation after this, but nothing of substance. It consisted mainly of Martyn Bedford talking in platitudes, telling me how proud I should be of the way I'd turned my life around, becoming almost a national figure in the process. I was a genuine spokesperson for the underpriviliged, he said.

'Don't worry, Mavis,' Martyn said, rising to his feet to indicate that this interview was now concluded. 'I won't stop trying to find out the full story. Bryony tells me that I should let it rest now, but I'll take it on as a private project. As soon as I find out anything more, I'll come back to you.'

Martyn never spoke to me on the subject again.

*

The years passed. As the turn of the Millennium was approaching, Mavis within me must have been well into her eighties. And still she wanted to keep working from the platform. It was an obsession with her, manifesting itself from somewhere deep within. Steve Charles, went along with it. Yes, I do realise I'm talking as if I were two people. But, by that time, that's the way I felt it was, even though Steve came to the fore less and less often.

Quite why this should be, I'm not sure. It may have been something to do with the simple fact that the central 'me' had lived within her frame for over twice as long as in Steve Charles's original life. The 'tenancies' of the egos of Jim Corcoran, Hubert Grey and Victor Smith had all been brief and uncomfortable in their different ways. Now they rarely troubled the pattern of my life. But I knew, that in some strange way, they were still there.

Eventually, though, even the Mavis element of me had to recognise that she was not indestructible. Several speaking engagements had been the subject of last-minute cancellations over the last few months. I knew Bryony Richards wouldn't stand in the way of a decision to call a halt to my demanding schedule.

Indeed, I was sure Bryony would welcome my acceptance of the inevitable. This was perhaps why I chose to tell her about it at what was to prove to be the last of our routine fortnightly meetings.

*

I hardly gave Bryony a chance to speak when she walked in that day. As soon as she'd taken her usual seat in my front parlour Helen, still my maid and general assistant, had poured each of us a half glass of Fino Sherry and left the room as usual. Neither Bryony nor I had taken so much as a sip from our drinks when I started to speak.

'Bryony,' I said. 'Today I want to dispense with our normal agenda. I have something important I want to tell you about.'

She looked surprised at this. I couldn't really think why. Our fortnightly meetings had become routine in the extreme. Bryony would start by handing me a list of my speaking engagements for the next two months. Neatly attached would be detailed notes on how she'd arranged to get me to and from those engagements. We'd briefly run through her plans, although Bryony had always thought of every detail.

There were rarely any surprises because we'd discussed each booking at a previous fortnightly meeting. Next, we'd talk about engagements for more than two months ahead. The whole process rarely took more than twenty minutes. We'd end with an hour or more of general chit-chat.

In truth, our fortnightly interactions had become more of a social event as the years passed. This was why I was surprised to see Bryony screwing up her features with concern now. She looked as nervous as I was feeling myself.

'Bryony,' I said. 'You look like you have something important you want to say yourself. Spit it out.'

'Well,' she said, 'I do have something on my mind, yes.' At first, she would say nothing further.

I thought immediately of Martyn Bedford. Was my friend pursuing some middle-aged dream of romance across the generations? Surely not? Bryony was far too sensible. But, no, Bryony started to speak on a quite different subject. It was the one that had been uppermost in my own thoughts.

'This is something we've talked about before,' she said at last. 'Today, I really want us to talk in earnest about it. Mavis, I've said many times before that you should reduce your heavy workload. Two or three stage appearances a month would be quite enough for you. This would be more than enough.'

I couldn't believe my ears. Here was Bryony saying exactly – no, not exactly – what

I had been so nervous about telling her. I'd been thinking it was time for me to stop altogether.

'Sorry to speak so plainly, Mavis, but I'm thinking of you. If you don't drastically reduce your programme in the way I've said, you'll have to find a new manager.'

I wanted to laugh. I wanted to cry. I wanted to explain everything to Bryony and squeeze my friend tightly. But I could do none of these things. There was a sudden darkening at the edge of my field of vision and my lips moved up and down, all but wordlessly. I managed to gasp out '…want… St Mary's…'

Even as these words left my lips, I had no clue as to why I was saying them. How could anyone else be expected to understand?

This whole process lasted only for seconds. Soon my vision faded altogether, and I felt myself pitching forward into the ourstretched arms of my friend Bryony.

[6] Bryony

This time the transition seemed to go peacefully and was free of confusion. One moment I was Mavis, at the sudden end of a long life. That life had, in ways I did not really understand, often been difficult, but in its last forty or so years it had been, if not entirely happy, at least materially successful.

Now the body of Mavis was lying in the arms of her friend and admirer, Bryony Richards, all at once become me. At this moment, I could feel Bryony's own grief mingling with my surprise – I can put it no stronger than this – at this abrupt change.

I, Stephen Charles, could appreciate this emotions of loss because he – or I – felt them, too. Mavis had been my host, if that was the way I should even describe it, for around forty years. In that time, I'd developed a genuine affection for her.

I wondered briefly if this seemingly smooth transition had been made possible by the nature of Mavis's death. Stephen Charles's original body had perished in a fearful accident, Jim Corcoran had died at the end of a rope in Wandsworth Prison, Victor Smith had been murdered. Hubert Grey's death may have been technically natural, but it had hardly been a peaceful one.

For a full fifteen minutes I looked down at Mavis's body with thoughts like these passing through my mind. Then, I all at once realised that I should call for help. Mavis was far beyond help, but this would have been the expected thing for me to do.

'Helen! Helen! Come quickly!'

Helen was upstairs on some domestic mission when I called. It was a few minutes before she entered the room but, as soon as she did, she took charge of the situation with her usual efficiency.

Soon the house was filled with ambulance men and others. As they lifted Mavis's body gently from my arms, I swear I could feel the last shreds of Bryony's personality being taken from me, too. I, Stephen Charles, was free for the first time since a dark, wet night in November 1959.

Or so I thought.

*

I was a rich man. Or, as the world saw me, a rich woman. Bryony had piled up considerable wealth over the years. Mavis, who'd accumulated even more, had left everything to Bryony in her will.

The only slight drawbacks I found to start with were purely practical ones. Stephen Charles had no clue as to exactly where Bryony now lived in Ealing since she'd recently moved to a plusher house.

Mavis had given up driving years before. Fortunately, I found a note of 'my' address in Bryony's pocket diary. This wasn't far from her own house or the one where I'd lived as Mavis. It was also close to the one where Hubert Grey, the churchman, had lived so many years before. And as I had, for a few days.

I solved the practical difficulties of transport by the simple means of employing a chauffeur. Bryony had always loved driving and, although people were puzzled at the explanation I gave for stopping with apparent suddenness – that Mavis's death had been too upsetting – they seemed to readily accept it.

There were other practical matters to deal with, too, like those presented by the multiplicity of passwords and account numbers we all had to live with, but I'd managed to solve most of these in crossword-puzzle fashion within a fortnight.

Martyn Bedford presented me with a wildly different sort of problem.

*

This I discovered at Mavis's funeral, just over a fortnight after her death. The old-fashioned burial was to be in a small churchyard close to my new – new to me – home in Ealing and I was able to dispense with the services of my chauffeur and walk to the service.

St Mary's was the last thing I had heard myself as Mavis saying. It seemed wholly the right thing to have the service in the old church. There were some problems with the new incumbent, who didn't know Mavis. He said, bluntly, that as far as he knew, she'd never set foot in his church, but a donation to funds put this minor matter right.

*

As I stood there at the graveside, next to Martyn, I realised I was becoming more and more disturbed by his presence. No, I should be honest. It was far more than this. I was becoming deeply, unstoppably physically attracted to him.

I tried to tell myself that this was the essence of Bryony, unexpectedly and strongly manifesting itself in this diminished form, but it shocked me to find how strong the physical longing was. There seemed to be nothing else of the old, strong, Bryony in evidence.

It was a Catholic service, as specified by Mavis in her will. All right, I have to say the will had really been specified by me, Steve Charles, years before. I must have had some vague thoughts of Jim Corcoran and Father Hubert Grey when I had the solicitor draw it up.

Before the priest was far into his service I suddenly became a welter of confused emotions.

Tears streamed down my cheeks. Part of these came from genuine grief at the passing of Mavis. The small congregation would have seen my outburst as Bryony's natural upset at her loss of Mavis.

But I knew that the greater part of my tears owed more to the confusion I knew at that moment. Where was the Bryony that Mavis had known for so long?

Martyn leaned over and grasped my shoulder firmly. He whispered in my ear:

'Don't worry, Bryony. You're not going to walk home from here, short as the distance might be. I'm going to look after you. I'll see you home.'

Martyn smiled down at me. My heart really did give a physical flutter. In that moment I knew, if I didn't already, exactly which part of Bryony's personality had survived this transition. In that moment, I was lost.

'Thank you,' I managed to say, in a weak voice. alien to anything I'd heard from Bryony's lips in all the years Mavis had known her.

'No sense in waiting and having you upset yourself further. We'll go to the car now.'

Martyn had taken full control of the situation. He firmly guided me down the churchyard path and out of the gate. Neither of us spared a backward glance for the small gathering at the graveside, even though in theory we were the chief mourners.

We soon passed through the few quiet streets leading to the house. As Martyn pulled up the car, I almost started to blub full force again. Thankfully, I managed to control myself.

Martyn was out of his side of the car in a flash and holding the passenger door open for me.

'Now I'm going to come in and make you a cup of tea. Although I don't share your view that tea has magical properties' – Martyn smiled broadly – 'I do think it's exactly the right thing for you at this moment.'

'No, no. I'll be fine. Honestly, I'll be OK. Don't worry.'

I said this too quickly. Martyn regarded me steadily.

'Well,' he said after a long moment's hesitation, 'perhaps you're right and it's best to try to get back to normal as soon as you can. Don't think twice before giving me a bell if you need to, mind. We're due to be seeing each other next week. Are sure you'll be OK for Monday?'

'Monday?'

'Yes. Our usual business meeting to start the week. I'll be at your place at the normal ten o'clock. Better allow for it to go on for a bit longer next week. We haven't been able to meet since Mavis died. Maybe we could just touch on the proposals I put to you as well? Things have changed for our business now.'

'Ten o'clock… Monday,' I recited.

I couldn't understand what was happening. Bryony's will was returning so assertively. No… I realised it was not her will exactly. It was just one element of it: her blind desire for Martyn Bedford.

'Right. You sure you'll be OK?'

I felt Martyn eyes upon me as I walked down the garden path. I unlocked the door and turned to wave to him. He waved back, smiling sympathetically. It was the last time I was to see any real sympathy from him.

*

Inside the house, I gave way to the floods of confusion already engulfing me. I made so much noise that Helen, working for me since Mavis's death, came in to see me in my grief. If only it was simple grief!

All those years before, Al had teased me as Steve, calling me a 'cock virgin'. Well, no matter how you looked at it, I was still a cock virgin. But now one with some extra, alarming, dimensions.

The despicable Victor Smith had tried to take me, whoever I was, in another direction, but his crude efforts in the brief time I'd occupied his body had been frustrated. They'd even led to his death by Mavis's hand.

For most of the last forty years I'd lived within women. The first of the two had seemingly been happy with celibacy.

The second, as I was now beginning to understand in a shadowy way, must have harboured a quiet desire for Martyn for years. Now it was surging to the surface. And there seemed to be nothing else of the true Bryony to keep it in check.

Unchecked, Bryony's urges were haunting me with a force frightening in its strength. Where did that leave me as Steve Charles? Indeed, where did it leave Bryony Richards, a strong woman now diminished in a way I could hardly begin to understand?

*

Sunday. Mavis's funeral had been on the Thursday. I was seeing Martyn tomorrow. I was still in utter confusion about my identity, far more so than in any of my previous lives. Most especially, I was in turmoil about my sexual identity.

How would I react to Martyn's presence with me in this house? Now I realised the reason why I'd been so anxious for him not to come in last Thursday was that I was beginning to feel sure I'd be sure to have made an old fool of myself as Bryony.

It probably would have been simpler if I'd done exactly this. That afternoon would have been embarrassing and the aftermath would have been painful for me, but at least I'd know where I was. I might even be able to make a start on rebuilding the wreckage this life was already becoming.

*

Martyn started the meeting, as if he was the senior in the business. In truth, that is exactly what he was. He was brisk and efficient: I was his open-mouthed acolyte.

In reply to my naïve question, Helen had told me there would be no sherry, nor even a coffee with Martyn. I couldn't help thinking how strongly this meeting contrasted with the cosy fortnightly chats Mavis and Bryony used to share.

'Then you'll have seen, Bryony,' Martyn was saying, 'why we now can't afford to postpone the changes I want a moment longer. Mavis always was the centrepiece of the agency division of our activities. That was the only aspect of our business you were much concerned with in a practical sense, if truth be told.'

He looked at me as if I were a fussy old maiden aunt.

'For some time now, she was inevitably far less effective as a money-spinner for Bryony Enterprises. You did well to have coaxed her along as you did. But you should have taken on more of my ideas earlier. Now the goose that laid the golden eggs for us has gone we need to diversify further. We need do it quickly'

Martyn smiled with his dismissive words. I was shocked. Not only because I had shared so many years with Mavis, but he seemed to be forgetting that the financial well-being of himself as well as the business owed everything to Mavis, even if she has been getting older as the years went by.

I managed to hold my tongue. Or was it Bryony who was holding my tongue? Instead, I asked about the proposals he had in mind. He'd spoken as if I should be familiar with them.

'What proposals?'

'How do you mean, "what proposals?" Those we've discussed many times in this forum, of course. The ones I set out in detail and sent you three weeks ago, woman. Don't tell me you didn't print the details out and bring them with you to our meeting?'

Martyn's tones were hardly those of a subordinate speaking to his boss.

'Oh, those proposals. Yes, I agree with everything you say. Go ahead.'

I said this in a foolish attempt to cover my stupid mistake. Of course, the two of them would have discussed matters in previous meetings. And I said it because Martyn was looking at me...

'Everything?'

Now it was Martyn's turn to look surprised.

'Yes, you go ahead.'

Martyn made a few rapid strokes on the keyboard of the silver mobile he always seemed to be holding in his left hand.

'You did read the bit about the necessary injection of our personal cash into the business, didn't you? That's three quarters of a million pounds in your case.'

I tried to control the shock his words had given to me. But I knew that, in life, Mavis had insisted that Bryony, as well as herself, keep her personal money separate from the business assets. With the bequest from Mavis, there would still be considerably more than three quarters of a million left in Bryony's bank accounts.

'I've read it all,' I lied.

'Great.' Martyn shrugged. 'That'll make things so much easier. As will me becoming a joint director with you to replace Mavis. You and I will start making some real money from now on, Bryony. I'm glad you're coming to see things my way at last.'

There was more, but it was all in this vein. Mavis had only been mentioned by way of being a lost business asset. Bryony's personal welfare not at all.

'Well,' said Martyn, rising from his seat. 'that went well. Took us less than an hour, too. I'll look after all the details. You'll only have a few things to sign. I'll let you know when. Next week, we'll again have something important to discuss. Looking forward to it, Bryony.'

So was I. But I knew our reasons were different.

*

There was sun streaming into my living room as Martyn entered. On what was for me only our second business meeting, he carried no sort of briefcase. Even his left hand was free of its burden of his mobile.

He took the seat close to mine and smiled the sunniest smile I'd ever seen from him. I at once lost my power of speech. What was wrong with me? I couldn't even trust myself to bid him good morning, so looked in his eyes and nodded demurely instead.

Martyn spoke first.

'No agenda this morning. Everything is going to our plan. This weekly business meeting is now a meeting of joint directors.'

In an almost reflex action, he reached for his mobile and looked briefly abashed when his empty hands met. He soon recovered his poise.

'We have only one agenda item to discuss,' he said. 'Paper and electronics would only get in the way of our discussion this time, don't you think?'

'Yes, Martyn,' I said.

I felt I had to say something, even though I had no real idea as to with what I was agreeing.

'Good. This matter really doesn't belong in the records of Bryony Enterprises. It is essentially personal between us.'

A personal matter?

'Now, let me ask you something to begin with. How long have we two been working together?'

'Well over twenty years. It must be.'

I remembered Bryony telling Mavis about that day.

'On the seventh of next month it will be twenty-two years.'

His expression became even more self-satisfied.

'As long as that?'

'As long as that,' Martyn echoed. 'And in that time, would you say I've done my level best for Bryony Enterprises?

Bryony Enterprises? Yes, that was still our business name.

'More than that, Martyn. For at least the last twenty years you've really been Bryony Enterprises. Not me.'

'You undervalue yourself, Bryony. For so long you nursed our most important asset along. This was our foundation: our anchor, so to speak. All I really did was keep the lesser stuff out of your hair. With a good degree of financially rewarding success, I will acknowledge.'

That was one way of looking at it, I suppose, even if a generous one to me.

'But times change, Bryony,' Martyn continued with hardly a pause. 'The changes we agreed last week will bring us far more up to date. In a year at most, the agency work will be no more than a minor part of what we do. Perhaps not even that. Now I'm joint director, everything will be so much easier.'

Here he paused for breath at last. But only for a moment.

'There is one thing more I need to ensure everything goes smoothly. This is the personal matter I spoke about. It's not strictly part of Bryony Enterprises activity at all.'

A personal matter? Could it be...?

'Oh?' was all I could manage to say.

'The weakness in my own position, Bryony, is that I have no real personal fortune of my own. I'm not complaining, mind. I'm hardly on my uppers. You've been more than generous to me over the years and my own wants never have been extravagant.'

'Then what...?'

'As I've intimated several times, those with whom we deal have to take more notice of me if I had real personal wealth behind me. I don't have that wealth, but you do. So-'

'Oh, Martyn!'

He was going to ask me to marry him! Like Steve Charles I, was a child of an earlier generation. This was the first thought that jumped into our curiously bound consciousnesses. There was no shadow of doubt in my mind that my money was the real attraction. But I'd looked after myself over the years and perhaps we'd be able to build a bridge over the twenty years between us?

'That's right,' Martyn said. 'I want you to make me the sole beneficiary of your will. Oh, I don't want any more money from you now. Your generous investment in the new Bryony

Enterprises will put us on the right road. We'll both make a lot of money from it.'

'I see.'

I was crushed. Martyn was seeing this purely as a financial matter. The money itself was not important, I acknowledged to myself. There was no one either Steve or Bryony wanted to leave assets to.

In fact, Bryony's sketchily returning memory told me that her existing will had been drawn up twenty-five years before, in favour of an animal charity. Assets had grown considerably since that time, but there had never seemed a need to change it.

Martyn, recovering from the first surprise I had ever seen him express, spoke again. There was a note of anxiety in his voice.

'You did understand what I was saying?'

'Martyn, can you give me a week to think this one through?'

As he left the room, I thought I detected the hint of a stoop in the way Martyn held his shoulders. This again was something new.

*

Over the next week I was in turmoil. Why had Martyn affected me so badly? Who was I now, anyway? Was I Steve Charles or Bryony Richards?

Or was I some awkward fusion of the two? Most of the time, up until now, Steve, in his quiet way, had been the leading personality. Now, some basic part of Bryony was taking the lead. In truth, her most elemental desires, rather than the business sense and strength she'd shown in life, were now assuming charge.

It was on Friday, while cooking some cannelloni in the plush kitchen, that I started to form a plan.

*

One of the first things I noticed about Martyn when he walked in for our third Monday morning meeting was that he was back to his habit of clutching his mobile. I had intended to be the first one to speak at this meeting, but he beat me to it.

'Well, Bryony, I hope you've done some serious thinking about my ideas over the last week. I have been thinking it through carefully. My decision is that if you want us to be simple business partners, then that's fine with me. It will mean Bryony Enterprises won't grow as fast as I hoped but grow it will'.

'The legal agreement you've already signed means that I can make all the necessary decisions without recourse to you. The additional financial investment you've made is non-reversible. In fact, I've already started to put it to work.'

I was astounded by his words. He had indeed been doing some thinking on his own account. This was the old, supremely confident Martyn. What he said next almost made the Bryony element of me cry out in anguish.

'These Monday morning meetings of ours take up valuable time. This is time that could be put to better use. So, this will be the last regular meeting. Don't worry, I'll arrange the occasional briefing and there'll be weekly – well, perhaps monthly will suffice – written reports.'

He started to rise from his seat, as if to bring the meeting to a close. The Bryony part of me almost screamed. She wanted to tell Martyn to take everything. But Steve remembered the plan from last Friday.

'But I haven't even had the chance to say anything yet!'

Martyn smirked. He actually smirked.

'There are only two possible answers to the proposal I made last week. One is yes and the other is no. You said no, or as good as, last week. Your face this morning tells me the answer is still no. Need we prolong the meeting?'

'There is a third way...'

The Bryony part of me wouldn't let me say more. She was hoping Martyn would guess what that third way was. He didn't even bother to try.

'Out with it then,' Martyn said impatiently. 'Come on. I have an important meeting in thirty minutes.'

'You could marry me,' I blurted out. 'I know enough about the law to say that any existing will usually become invalid upon the marriage of one of its makers. We can tidy things up as necessary after our marriage.'

'Marry you? Me?'

He was stunned. What I said had come as a complete surprise to him.

'I know there are so many years between us, Martyn. But we can learn together. And you know I won't stand in the way of your ambitions in business'.

He still didn't answer. He still looked stunned by my suggestion.

'Do you really think I'm too old for you, Martyn?'

Here he glanced in my direction fully for the first time. His expression was not an unkind one, so it seemed.

'It's not that, Bryony. It's simply that there could be… complications…. I'd need to think how we can make this one work.'

The old Martyn was back, seeing what I'd said as no more than another business proposal, weighing up the pros and cons. But at least he hadn't dismissed what I'd said out of hand. To be honest, this was what I'd expected.

'Do you want to meet again next week?' I tried to inject a little levity into a situation I didn't really understand. 'Only one item on the agenda.'

I tried to smile. Martyn couldn't or wouldn't see the joke. He seemed still to be treating my proposal as a business proposition.

'No need, no need. I have the beginnings of an idea. We could make it all work.'

Bryony's heart leaped within me. The desperate suggestion hadn't been rejected out of hand.

'What about the meeting you mentioned?'

'He can wait. This is more important. I'll ring him in a moment. Look, I'll go and get Helen to make us a cup of coffee... no, I'll make the coffee myself. It'll give me time to dot the i's and cross the t's on the plan that's coming to me. Back in no more than ten.'

Martyn rose from his seat. I tried to read his expression, but it was unfathomable. Neither angry nor happy, just thoughtful.

For the first time in his life, Martyn was going to have a cup of coffee with me. Not only that, but he was going to make it himself.

*

'Good coffee?'

'Yes. Lovely.'

I was lying.

Martyn liked a strong, milkless and unsweetened Americano. He'd made both of our coffees in that way. There was no jug or sugar-bowl on the table. If he'd have asked me, I'd have told him I preferred a weak Latte and hoped there'd be some coconut milk in the kitchen.

He watched me sipping my coffee. It was far too strong for me, but I tried not to show my distaste. Long before I was half-way down the cup, he'd finished his own and replaced it on the table.

Three-quarters of a cup was all I could manage before I had to give up the unequal struggle and follow suit. Anyway, Martyn was already showing signs of impatience.

'Here's what we do,' he said without any kind of preamble. 'We will get married, but there are certain things we have to do. You will need to follow my instructions to the letter.'

He didn't give me a chance to say anything. This was exactly the way he used to put forward his business proposals.

'Over the next month, you should start calling in to the office to talk to me, in the way you used to do all those years ago. None of the people you knew at that time are still there, so you'll have to work hard to become a familiar face to those who work for me now.'

'This shouldn't be so hard to achieve. They all know your name. Some of them have been working under it for years. Now they'll have a face to go with the name. It should be a friendly face, too. Social chit-chat is what we need from you, Bryony. You've always been good at that sort of thing.'

This was how he saw Bryony, then. He had entirely forgotten that not too many years ago I was an eager young businessperson, too. But I hope I'd been one with a human face.

'Let them get to know the boss's new wife, eh? Well, I'll have plenty to talk about with them there.'

'*No!* No, Bryony. On no account. The one thing you must never do is talk about our impending marriage.'

The puzzled, hurt look on my face told Martyn he'd been too quick to say this. Was he already becoming ashamed of his bride-to-be?

'Look, Bryony. Try to see things from the perspective of the staff.' His tone became gentler. 'Merely seeing you for the first time will be a lot for them to take in. We don't want them to think too many momentous changes are afoot. Over the next six months, I want to keep them all on my side – our side.'

One month? Six months? What did Martyn have in mind now?

'I don't know why six months should be important to our future together, Martyn.'

'Then let me explain,' he said, still in a quiet voice. 'I'm trying to do exactly that now, if only you'd let me.'

He fell silent.

I'd been reprimanded, though had no real idea why. The Steve element of me, weakening all the time now, wanted to protest, but

Bryony's new personality made me nod a meek acceptance.

Martyn continued to hold his silence for what seemed a long time to me. At last, his features relaxed and he resumed speaking.

'Now, as I said, I want you to call into the office to see me a number of times – say at least seven or eight over the next month. We'll pre-arrange these times, but it'll look as if you've called in on-spec and I won't be able to see you straight away.'

'This'll give you plenty of opportunity to talk to the staff. As I said, there must be no mention of our marriage – or indeed any part of our personal life together – except in one important respect. I want them to know how much you're looking forward to taking a back seat in the business and retiring back to your roots in North Wales.'

'But I don't want to retire to North Wales. I've never been there in my life! It's by your side I want to be.'

Martyn laughed.

'I am trying to explain my plan to you, Bryony. You won't really be retiring to North

Wales. What good would that be for me? I may be a director alongside you, but I have only a five percent financial stake in Bryony Enterprises. After six months we'll marry. We'll each play our full parts in the company.'

'But I don't want to go to North Wales for any time at all!'

'You won't be going to North Wales. That's what you'll say to the people in the office. You'll actually be going to Southwold, in Suffolk. After six months I'll come up and marry you there.'

It all sounded so complicated to me.

'But I still don't understand...'

'Bryony, you're full of questions. I have only one question for you. Do you trust me?

Steve Charles had a thousand questions in his mind. But Bryony was the one who answered.

'Yes.'

*

The six months I spent alone in Southwold were purgatory. Walking on the beach seemed about the only thing to do. One day in mid-

October, I took sandwiches and walked all the way to Dunwich.

I resolved to do more serious walking like this, so as to get myself fit for Martyn's arrival, but this resolution faded as the Winter progressed.

Martyn's arrival… In truth I could think of little else. It was thoughts about this that finally convinced me I'd somehow become two personalities within one body. The Bryony part of me, now by far the stronger, yearned for the day of Martyn's arrival. He'd told me this would be on the last day of the following March.

To Bryony this seemed a lifetime away. The Stephen Charles part of me, who day by day was becoming the weaker element within me, was terrified at the prospect of the much-postponed sex.

Then, at mid-day on Friday 30th March 2001 – I know the date exactly – Martyn telephoned. I was surprised because he'd previously done so earlier on that same week, on the Monday.

'Bryony?'

The Steve part of me was banished to silence as soon as I heard Martyn's voice.

'Martyn? Is it really you? You phone so rarely, and we only spoken earlier in the week. You'd only rung me twice before in the period since last August. And you told me not to get in touch with you. You certainly wasted your money when you had this phone installed. It's hardly been used. I could have as easily have used my mobile.'

I could sense Martyn's cold anger as these words tumbled out.

'You're babbling again, woman. I've explained all this to you, carefully. As I told you, I didn't want you to use a mobile at all. I couldn't leave you in Southwold without a telephone, could I? You did follow my instructions on the use of the landline, didn't you?'

'Yes,' I said. 'To the letter. I only used it on that one occasion to ring the number in Halesworth you gave me, when I needed a plumber. There's been no need for me to use it for anything else. You instructed me not to ring you at home or at work if you remember.'

I'd been puzzled by some of Martyn's instructions and didn't always understand his explanations, but the last thing I wanted was to annoy him again. I was more than half-afraid that he was going to say he wasn't coming over, tomorrow after all.

'Good,' he said. 'We're all set for tomorrow, then. Our big day.'

I was so relieved when he said this. He could have said anything now. When I answered, I tried to keep the breathless excitement out of my voice.

'And all the papers you told me to make sure of have been already packed and are ready to go. I'll be waiting for you at eleven o'clock, exactly as you said.'

'That's why I'm phoning now. Can you be ready at nine o'clock instead?'

'Nine o'clock? That's early.'

'It's hardly crack of dawn stuff.'

'I was only thinking it would be early for you, Martyn. Where are you now?'

There was a pause at the other end of the line. Then Martyn spoke.

'Suffolk. Place called Blyth.'

'Blyth? That's only a few miles away from Southwold. Can't you come over now? We'll have our own little celebration here.' I felt a warm glow as I said this. 'The formalities can wait until tomorrow.'

I could sense his annoyance at the other end of the line. But Martyn didn't sound too annoyed when he answered.

'Bryony,' he said. 'We went through all this while both of us were still in London. I told you we'd need to wait another six months with you up here. I tried to explain to you: this is a deeply held religious belief of mine. When we walk out of Southwold Township Office in the morning, we'll be husband and wife. Not before.'

Husband and wife. Bryony liked the sound of that. Steve Charles and his fears counted for nothing.

*

'I'm so looking forward to our honeymoon after the marriage registration at Southwold Township office,' said Martyn, as he held open the door of his plush new BMW for me.

'Not as much as I am, I'll bet.' 'Seems like I've been waiting for this moment all my life. Still, now we're a bit earlier than we thought we'd be. We can come back here for an hour before we head north. Just long enough to…*you* know.'

Martyn climbed in, taking the driver's side seat beside me. Then he turned to me and fixed me with a stern look.

'Bryony, I've told you this before. Stop trying to pretend you're a teenager. We're going to do this properly. Our honeymoon will be in the village I was brought up in, near Alnwick. That's over 300 miles away. It will take us the best part of six hours to drive there, all the way up the A1. Now, buckle up.'

Martyn didn't say '…buckle up and shut up'. He may as well have done. He hardly spoke until we were well past Norwich, even when we were in Southwold Township Office. This was where I became a married woman for the only time in my life. I well remember the first time he said anything that he didn't have to.

We were speeding along the A17, near a small place called Byard's Leap in Lincolnshire. I remember thinking I was making Bryony's Leap. Martyn's eyes left the road for a full two seconds as he turned to me and spoke. A pleasant smile was written across his features, despite the edginess that had grown sharper between us over the last few hours.

'Happy?'

This was all he said. Was I? Whether I was or not, I had to keep making that leap.

*

'The house is more than a bit old and run-down looking,' I said.

He looked at me. His expression was unfathomable.

'It is old. This is where I was born and brought up. This building is a full century-and-a-half older than me. When it came on the market eight years ago, I couldn't resist buying it. For sentimental reasons. You, more than most people, should understand this sort of thing.'

I looked across at Martyn as if for the first time. In all the time I'd known him, he'd never spoken of sentiment. Did I know him at all?

'Perhaps we could come back in the morning and take a proper look?

'Bryony. I've just been driving for six hours. It's another fifteen miles on to Alnwick. I need a rest. I'll make you a cup of tea. And there's something I need to tell you.'

'You're not going to say you've changed your mind,' I tried to laugh. 'You're too late. I'm Mrs Bryony Bedford now.'

He reached over and grasped my hand warmly, if briefly.

'And I wouldn't want it any other way. Come on.'

Martyn unbuckled his seat belt and stepped out of the car smartly. I scrambled after him. He strode purposefully as he strode up the long, overgrown garden path, without once checking behind him to see if I was following.

Closer to, the house looked even more ancient and abandoned. The green paint on the plain, wooden front door looked as if it had been applied decades ago. Every one of the windows was streaked with ancient grime.

Martyn extracted a large key from his pocket. When he turned it in the lock, it made a loud clunking noise. He opened the heavy door.

'*Entrez!*'

He said this while making a theatrical gesture with his hand. I shrank back.

'You first,' I said.

Martyn laughed.

'Don't worry,' he said. 'I'm not going to offer to carry you over the threshold. Anyway, this old place is hardly going to be your new home.'

'Then why stop here?'

'I've told you,' Martyn said. 'I need a break before I drive another mile. And I have something important to tell you about.'

I followed him in. The house seemed even tinier inside. The inside walls had been crudely painted years before with yellowing emulsion, now all but faded. There were only a few bleached and greying floormats, two faux-leather armchairs, and a small wooden table for furnishings in this, what must be the main room.

'Were you really brought up as a child here, Martyn?'

'For my first eight years, yes. That door on the left leads to my bedroom. Mine, my brother's, and my mother's. Then we moved to Alnwick itself.'

I didn't dare ask about his father. He'd never spoken about his family before.

'Where does that other door lead to?'

'That's the kitchen. And it's about time I made that cup of tea for you.' He saw the look of alarm on my face. 'Don't worry. I've been too busy down south to get the place cleaned up and refurnished, but I do have some fresh tea bags and a set of new cups and saucers in the kitchen. Take a seat while I'm there. Make yourself comfortable.'

I could do the first thing but knew I could never do the second in this house.

*

'Good tea?' said Martyn, from the seat opposite mine.

I nodded and smiled. It really was good tea. I'd added a dash of sugar and a generous amount of milk from the jug Martyn had brought in on the tray with the elegant cups. They formed a matching set and were at odds with our spartan, grubby surroundings.

'Now,' I said. 'What's this important thing you wanted to tell me?'

'Enjoy your tea first.'

Martyn watched my face eagerly as I sipped the rest of my cup. This was very off-putting. It was a relief when I was able to drain the cup and return it to the table.

'Finished!'

He said nothing at first. Then he looked at me with a serious expression on his face.

'This is a very complicated story,' he at last said. 'I hardly know where to start. With an apology, I suppose.'

'Apology? An apology for what?'

'Yes,' Martyn said. 'An apology is the only word for it. Do you remember, all those years ago, when you gave me a project to find out more about Mavis's earlier life for her?'

That was years in the past. I was puzzled.

'Well, I never did report back to you properly. I'm sorry.'

'You did report back to me. We discussed it at the time, as I remember. Mavis spent the years from the end of the Second World War tramping, as far as we know, along the Thames in London. Nobody would be able to find out much about that. So I was hardly surprised when you couldn't find so little about her earlier life.'

He looked blankly at me. It was impossible to gauge what his feelings were.

'When I reported back to you, I already had a good indication that during the later war years she lived with an American Air Force sergeant. I should have told you this and what it was pointing me towards – the real story of the woman. I'd already started to investigate this as a private project of my own. The more I uncovered, the more fascinated I became. It's taken me all these years to find out as much as I have.'

I was frankly confused.

'Well,' I said, ' to have her lover disappearing back to the USA must have been hard for her to take. Many British girls would have experienced the same thing.'

He looked at me steadily.

'Now, how did you know this American went back to the USA?'

'I… er… it was a guess. This was what happened to a lot of British girls after the war. It's common knowledge. Some became GI brides. Many didn't.'

'Don't bluster, woman,' he said. 'I know much more about what happened than you seem to realise. The American sergeant episode must have been hard to take, yes. Perhaps it was the final straw for our Mavis, but I'm sure it was what happened earlier in the war that really mattered.'

'Earlier in the war? But we know nothing about Mavis' earlier life.'

Martyn looked at me. His eyes were hard and unsympathetic.

'You might not. At least, that's what Mavis always used to say. It may disappoint you to know I've been able to put most of the story together. It's taken me years of difficult research. I haven't told a soul about it until now, Bryony. Now I'm going to tell you everything I know. You already know much more than you've let on. And you never breathed a word of what you knew to me.'

What did he know? What was he going to tell me? I have to admit I panicked.

'Martyn, I swear to you I didn't know anything about Mavis's life before the war. Nor did she know anything herself.'

'Perhaps neither of you were aware of the full story. But you did understand something important. If you'd told me about it, this would have led me to unravelling the whole thing years before I at last managed to do it.'

'If I'd told him'. Surely he meant if Mavis had told him? I was growing frightened at the way Martyn was speaking.

'Now,' he said, 'are you going to shut up and listen while I tell the whole fantastic story to you?'

There didn't seem to be any answer to him. He seemed so sure of himself. All I could do was nod meekly.

'In the thirties and forties, Mavis was a young girl living in North Ruislip, a suburb on the western edge of London. It's been swallowed up by the city now, like so many other places.'

North Ruislip? That was a familiar name.

'Mavis Charles, still only nineteen before the Second World War, had an unofficial fiancé at that time. Neither set of parents knew anything about it, but the couple had the firm intention of getting married as soon as they could. They'd even selected the church – St Mary's in North Ruislip. Not the one in Ealing, where the priest, Hubert Grey, later went.'

He smiled when he saw my surprised expression at hearing this name.

'Oh yes, I do know all about Father Grey. I was very thorough in my investigation. Shame I can only now share the full facts with you.'

So Father Grey was then the incumbent at St Mary's in North Ruislip? Had Mavis somehow remembered this at the moment of her death? Had I arranged for her burial in the wrong churchyard?

'Mavis's fiancé was a very promising athlete and was thought to be a likely gold medal winner in the 1940 Olympics, due to be held in Tokyo.'

'But-'

'Yes, I can guess what you were going to say. There were no Olympic Games held in Japan. They were rescheduled to Helsinki because of Japanese military aggression in China. In the event, there were no Olympic Games held in 1940 at all because of the World War. The Helsinki Olympics didn't take place until 1952 and those in Tokyo not until 1964.'

I was mystified. This was all new information to me, but what did any of it have to do with Bryony or Mavis?

Martyn stopped speaking for a moment and studied my face intently.

'You're either doing a brilliant job of pretending, or you really don't know. The Olympic stuff is in the history books, but what if I told you that Mavis's fiancé's name was Jim

Corcoran? Would that jog your creaking memory?'

'Jim Corcoran? The man who was hanged for a murder he didn't commit?'

Martyn gave a derisory snort of laughter.

'Still trying to pretend, Bryony? Well, you have it your way for a bit longer. The important thing for Mavis is that budding athlete Jim took it into his head to save the World. It was in big trouble at that time if you know your modern history. He gave up his athletics, his girl Mavis, and everything else, just to join the army with his mates, Dennis Smith and Tommy Barker.

'The boys didn't see any real action until May 1940 when, like so many others, they struggled to get off Dunkirk Beach. By then, the three heroes had teamed up with a fourth soldier, who came from Parva-vale, near to where they lived in North Ruislip. His name was Alan Milgram. Ring any bells with you?'

'Alan Milgram?' I echoed, stupidly.

Martyn looked at me contemptuously.

'Ah,' he said. 'At last, we have a name that means something to that ageing head of yours. You should know all the names I've just given you, apart maybe from Tommy Barker. He didn't get off the beach. You have met his son, though. Ken Barker, he's called.'

This name I also knew but by then my head was spinning and I couldn't at first think from where. Martyn was studying my features and smiling.

'I'm going too fast for your old brain to keep up, obviously. What we'll do is give it an hour or so to start ticking into life. I have some important business calls to make. This I'll do from the kitchen. I'll be back later with another cup of tea, to see if that coaxes some life into it. I have a lot to tell you yet. Do try to understand what I've told you so far, Mrs Bedford.'

'Do we have any biscuits?' I don't know why I said this. It was so inane.

'No biscuits.'

Martyn picked up the tea tray and walked towards the door leading to the kitchen. I felt such a fool. And my thoughts were so confused after the things I'd heard.

*

Martyn rose, picked up the tray and its contents, then walked over to the kitchen door without a backwards glance at me. He unlocked the door and went inside, locking it behind him.

I listened for kitchen noises. Instead, a few minutes later, I heard a door being pulled closed at the back of the house. Next, I heard Martyn's footsteps crunching briskly on the gravel path around the house. Then a key was turned in the front door lock. The footsteps receded again, and I heard Martyn's car engine starting. I was alone.

I jumped up and tried all three doors in the room. Bedroom, kitchen, and front door, all had been locked from the other side. There were only two small windows in this room. Both were barred and locked.

What was Martyn doing? He'd said he was going to the kitchen. Why was he going off in his car? Was he going to leave to die alone in this dismal house?

*

For an hour, all I could do was sit there in a funk. Images of medieval corpses being found decades after they'd been walled up passed before my eyes. This ancient house was truly isolated. No one would have any reason to come to it. I felt exactly as if I had been bricked into its walls.

I slumped back in the chair, turning over in my mind the things Martyn had said. He'd mentioned Dennis Smith and Tommy Barker. Who were they?

'*Bernie and Den were in the card school. They worked with me in the Parva-vale wallpaper factory. So did Al – Alan Milgram.*' The voice sounded in my head, as if it came in an answer from nowhere. It was spoken in a voice I heard less and less often – that of Steve Charles…

And then there was Ken Barker… only now did I remember this was the name of the driver of Father Hubert Grey's car. This poor young man had, I'd been told, been briefly arrested for Father Grey's murder. Just a moment – who'd told me this? And had it been me they'd told? I began to doubt my sanity.

At the moment my thoughts were beginning to get out of control, I heard the noise of a car pulling up at the back of the house – Martyn had returned!

I listened to the progression of sounds: the car door being closed, the light tread as he approached the house, the characteristic humming under his breath. I expected to hear his footsteps on the gravel path around the house as he walked to the back door.

They didn't come. Instead, I heard a key turn in the heavy front door. Martyn entered – he was smiling, as if he was returning from a normal errand.

'Decided to take pity on you after all,' he said, holding up a shiny red paper packet. 'Thought I'd go out to get you some biscuits to have with your tea.'

'I love biscuits.'

It seemed a stupid thing to say. For a moment I even allowed myself to think Martyn was settling down into some sort of normality.

'One moment, Bryony. I'll go out to the kitchen to make you more tea in a moment. But you'll have had some thinking time while I've been gone. Did you make any sense of all those names I was throwing at you before I went?'

Why was he asking this? How did he
know who Den and Al and all the others were,
anyway? Martyn was far younger than me. But I
answered his question in a straightforward way.

'I know who three of them were at least.
They all worked in a factory in Parva-vale a
long time ago. But the name Tommy Barker
means nothing to me. I'm not entirely sure of
that of Jim Corcoran, either.'

The thoughts of Steve Charles came to me
once again, even as I spoke: *'Jim Corcoran was
hanged for my murder. He didn't do it. My
death was a pure accident.'*

Martyn looked at me suspiciously. My
expression must have changed as this thought
came to me.

'You either have a leaky memory or
you're a good liar – some of the time. I've just
told you that Tommy Barker didn't make it off
Dunkirk Beach. Are you really still trying to tell
me you don't know who Jim Corcoran was?'

What should I say now?

'I think I may have heard the name.'

It sounded so lame.

'You *think*? After the war, Alan Milgram – Al – found Den and his friend Bernie jobs in the wallpaper factory near his home in Parvavale. They both moved to the place from North Ruislip and lived there until they died. Starting to remember more now?'

Martyn chortled, as if he were telling the best joke in the world.

'Oh. I should have mentioned. You'll like this one. Den found Stephen Charles – you'll know that name, my love – a job in the wallpaper factory when the boy left school in the nineteen-fifties. Al was furious. He was all the angrier when Bernie invited Steve to play in the card school. This was Al's favourite thing in the week.'

How could, I, Bryony, remember these things? But images were starting to form in my mind. These were of scenes like me pushing a broom around the factory floor, thrusting my timecard into the metal clock contraption on the wall and registering my attendance with a thump in its top every morning. Most of all, I saw before my eyes coins, notes, and playing cards on a table underneath clouds of blue-grey cigarette smoke.

These weren't my memories: they were more of those from Steve Charles. After a period of near dormancy, his personality was re-emerging strongly again. Who was I?

'Wake up, Dolly Daydream. I'll go right back to the beginning, to 1938, when Mavis Charles' boyfriend took it into his head to put the World right. He joined the army, along with his mate, Den. Tommy Barker had already signed up. He must have been an even bigger mug than Jim..

'As I said, the first time they saw real action was in Dunkirk. It wasn't long before this they'd met Al. He hung around with them, but the other three never really accepted him'.

'The other three never really accepted me'. These had been the last words on the lips of Al himself. But he'd spoken those words to Mavis about twenty years ago. Was her personality also now re-emerging more strongly?

'I'm not going to repeat all this, woman. Pay attention, will you? Anyway, Dunkirk was an unmitigated disaster. The miracle was that so many soldiers' lives were saved. Our heroes' unit was especially badly hit.

'Mavis's boyfriend really tried to show himself to be a hero on that beach. He went back to save his best friend – Tommy Barker his name was. He managed to carry him back to the others.'

Martyn laughed shortly.

'Only Tommy died as Jim Corcoran brought him back. He'd been carrying a corpse! Then he found that Den was also missing. Somebody said he'd last been seen with Tommy Barker. Jim only jumps up and runs back to where he'd found Tommy. The bloody fool! Could have got himself killed. May as well have done, really. His life changed after that day.'

Martyn shook his head wonderingly. It looked to me as if the things he was talking about were entirely beyond his understanding. Then he continued to speak, much slower now.

'He nearly did get himself killed, too. No one knows exactly what happened, but he must have found Den lying on the beach somewhere because, almost half an hour later, they spotted him stumbling back with Den across his shoulders, exactly in the way he'd been carrying Tommy earlier.

'Then, before Jim and Den reached their unit, a shell or something exploded near them. They were both thrown to the ground. Some of the blokes in their unit ran out to get them. They all thought the two of them were dead, but the soldier boys were only unconscious and wounded.'

Martyn shook his head again. I could see he had no idea of how unthinkingly brave men could be on a battlefield. This clever – too clever – man would do nothing himself without a careful calculation.

'In fact,' he continued. 'Den was the first to regain consciousness in some sort of fashion, although he'd been well out of it since before Jim had rescued him and had no idea what had happened to him.'

Martyn's eyes were filled with horrified wonder at what he was telling me. I felt the need to say something.

'Some story that. How do you know all this?'

Martyn became indignant.

'It is *not* a story. It's what happened. And I know because I made a point of finding out. And I did it without the help you could have given me years ago. If you give me a chance, I'll tell you. I haven't yet come to the really important part'.

I knew it would be unwise to interrupt again. But how on Earth could Martyn know the detail of what had happened in 1940, on a beach in northern France? All I could do was nod, with what I hoped was an expression of contrition rather than puzzlement on my face.

'Al – Alan Milgram,' Martyn continued, 'had taken no part in any of this. It seems that he and Jim had taken a dislike to each other from the first. But when Jim and Den were back with the unit, it was Al made a point of being the one to go over to look after them both.

'This meant he was the first one to speak to either of them. Den of course knew nothing of what had happened, but neither did Jim – all his recent memories had been wiped out by the shell explosion.

'Al filled Jim's head with stories about how he himself had been the rescuer of Den and how he'd been the one who had tried hardest to save Tommy. He convinced Jim that Tommy might have lived if only Jim had shown more bravery. The sly bugger promised Jim that he'd never tell the truth about what had happened.

'Al told me all this himself. Jim, poor old sod, was ashamed of what he'd done, or really, what he thought he'd failed to do.'

But something about this didn't add up. An image was dredged from my memory – from the memory of Steve Charles. Jim *had* been recognised as the one to save Den. I couldn't prevent myself from shouting:

'Jim Corcoran *had* been awarded the Victoria Cross for his actions. He'd been awarded the Victoria Cross for it! I've seen the medal for myself!'

I'd seen it myself, or at least a photograph of it, through Jim Corcoran's eyes. Or were they Steve Charles's eyes? No longer was I sure. For no good reason, I even remembered the date when this was: 25th November 1959. Bryony was just a few years old then. My head was spinning.

Martyn looked at me mockingly.

'Yes, and I know exactly how you may have come to see it, too. It pays to have contacts in the police. Even if you often have to pay for them.'

He laughed mirthlessly.

'I was never able to track the medal down myself, all those years later. I first heard about it from Trevor Carruthers. I wish you'd told me what you knew. You could have saved me a lot of time.'

Trevor Carruthers? Who was he? I was too frightened to ask Martyn. But he gave me the answer, anyway.

'You wouldn't know anything about Trevor Carruthers. He was a young officer in the neighbouring unit at Dunkirk. He saw it all. His report was the thing that earned Jim his medal. His version of events – I suppose someone like you would call it "the truth" – became the official one.

'But he never had the chance to speak to Jim about what happened. Forever after, Jim believed what Al had told him. Carruthers was severely injured himself not too long afterwards and right out of it for years. When I spoke to him years later, he was an old codger going on about his war wound.'

In that moment, the last shreds of my love – or, should I say, Bryony's strange blind desire – for Martyn were shattered.

'I promised the old soldier I'd tell Jim about it. You could say I'm doing that now, in a manner of speaking, through you. Sorry I'm a bit late about doing it.'

He smiled as he said this. I said nothing. What would have been the point?

'Anyway,' Martyn continued, 'what really mattered was that Jim carried on believing what Al had told him on that beach. Most of all, he carried the guilt of his friend Tommy Barker's death for the rest of his days.

'As soon as he could after Dunkirk – this was a few years, mind – he returned to active service and was sent to Belgium. After his discharge in 1946, Poor Jim rather went off the rails a bit. Pity, really, because years later he found out he had a young son.'

'A son?'

'Yes. You know him well – very well, in fact. His name was Stephen Charles. Young Steve could have done with a bit of paternal guidance, too. His mother, Mavis had lost her way a bit herself before then. The kid had no chance.'

Jim and Mavis were Stephen's parents? *My* parents?

'Lot to take in girl, yeah? I'll go and make you that cup of tea now, shall I? And you can have as many biscuits as you like. That'll make you feel better, eh?'

Martyn rose to his feet, showily picking up the shiny red packet of biscuits. But, instead of then walking towards the kitchen door, he returned to the front door and locked it with excessive display. Only afterwards did he go to the kitchen door, unlock it, and then lock it again from the other side when he'd passed through.

Not once did he spare the briefest glance in my direction.

*

It was a full twenty minutes before he emerged from the kitchen. They were the longest twenty minutes of my life – *my lives*. How could Bryony have been so stupid? Yes, Bryony. Hers had been just one of the six personalities clamouring for attention within me.

Stephen Charles now had the strongest voice again, or at least seemed to be the only one with the capacity for some sort of logical thinking. Jim Corcoran was the saddest. Father Hubert Green expressed a different kind of mournful regret. Victor Smith supplied a background of obscene grumbling. Mavis seemed to be baffled by everything.

When he unlocked the kitchen door and returned, Martyn carefully put the tray down on the table between us, exactly as if we were in polite society. The tray bore two cups and saucers, a jug of milk, and a large, decorated plate I'd not before seen. Upon this, numerous biscuits had been carefully arranged.

'Thought you deserved these while I tell you the rest of the story,' he said.

'Martyn, I don't want to hear any more.'

'Ah, but you must. I've lived with it for years. I couldn't tell anyone else, could I? They wouldn't believe me, for a start. I could hardly believe it myself at first. Enjoy your tea. I've made it exactly the way you like it.'

Now he was beaming at me. I was entirely sure he was mad.

'Martyn, please. Bryony Enterprises is yours. Just let me go now.'

He looked at me in surprise.

'Bryony Enterprises is a total irrelevance. Well, it is even more so now I've invested most of its assets in a real project. Anyway, you don't think I've worked so hard for all these years just for a bit of dosh, do you? Drink up your tea, there's a good girl.'

I picked up the cup, and in almost a trance stirred in my preferred four heaped spoons of sugar. Then I carefully added some milk. The tea tasted good, even though I could guess what else the cup might contain.

'You must know much of the rest of the story yourself,' he said. 'You could have saved me a lot of work by telling me what you did know. Still, perhaps some of its subtleties might have escaped you, so it might be just as well I did my own investigation the hard way.

'Among the many things I did – you wouldn't believe some of things I had to do – it became my life, Bryony, I'm telling you – was to track down and interview Will French, one of Jim Corcoran's guards in Wandsworth Prison.'

Here he paused, almost as if expecting a round of applause. The man French's name sounded faintly familiar, although I couldn't at first think why. All I could do was put on what I thought was a look of appreciation and nod meekly. This seemed to satisfy Martyn and he charged on with his rapid explanation.

'This turned out to be the crucial step. It was Will French who first put me onto this Ka business when he told me of Jim's fascination with a book about Ancient Egyptian beliefs.'

Ka business? Just how much did Martyn know? My head started to reel. Martyn cast a look of satisfaction in my direction. He'd seen the change in my expression.

'Before that time,' he said, 'I had been vaguely thinking some sort of multiple personality psycho-business must be involved. The truth was altogether more fantastic. That was when I decided that I wanted this for myself.'

'Yes, but it's…' I wasn't sure what I wanted to say.

Martyn continued breezily, now almost ignoring my presence.

'He was a greedy old sod, that Will French. I had to try to convince him that I was researching Jim's life and there'd somehow be money in it for him. The only way I could do that was by laying out some readies for him. This did the trick, though.

'He used a contact at the prison – a grandson, I think it was – to get hold of the book for me that Jim had read all those years before. It was still in the prison library, and the passages that had caught his imagination still had Jim's pencil markings against them. They were the really vital thing. And they'd been under French's nose years before. He hadn't even guessed at what he'd seen. Some people, eh?'

Martyn paused once more. I said nothing. What could I say?

'Anyway, at the same time I was doing all this research work, I even managed to start repair my finances in a small way. True, I have to admit that my schemes were on the fringe of legality, or even over its borders, but I made a start. Martyn Bedford will be back. Martyn Bedford will be back in a big way.

'I'm sure you'll know all about that dark night back in 1959 when Steve Charles had his fatal accident. Jim Corcoran was hanged for it, although I soon found out he'd played no part in the boy's death. After all, Jim had only moved back to North Ruislip to be near his newly discovered son.'

Martyn looked hard at me, as he emphasised the last few words.

'His son...' I murmured.

'Yes. I rather thought you'd have missed this bit. But now I'm pleased to be telling you about the most important thing. This was, you see, that when Our Jim went off to do his hero bit for his country, he'd left his girl, Mavis Charles, pregnant. Oh, yes, in some weird way you'd got her name right later.'

'So, Mavis was...'

Martyn smiled, showing his even white teeth.

'Now you have it exactly right. Mavis was Stephen's mother and Jim was his father. Jim didn't find out until years later that he even had a son because of Mavis's breakdown.'

Pleasure was written across his features as he spoke. He was enjoying my misery. *Our* misery.

'Jim couldn't even accept that he'd actually been a hero at Dunkirk. He'd saved Den's life and did his best to save that of his best friend, Ken Barker's father.'

Every one of the voices within me was clamouring.

'Please Martyn – no more. I don't want to hear more.'

'You may not want it, but you're going to have it while what you've drunk does its work. This tea won't be as good for you as you might have thought, but it will be better than Plan B.'

He gave a look of satisfaction, exactly as if he'd told a well-received joke.

'I hope you don't think I'd have brought you here without a Plan B for seeing you off, do you? I have a nice shiny pistol in my pocket.

'The only things are that with Plan B there'd be more cleaning to do than washing up a few cups. That greedy old Dr Fischer – he'll be here in an hour – would want even more money for his silly piece of paper, too. FINISH YOUR TEA!'

Martyn shouted this last with such force that I immediately picked up my cup and drained half of it. Then I whimpered, involuntarily.

'Bit too late for that, Bryony, don't you think? I couldn't believe it when I uncovered the truth. How the essence of Stephen Charles jumped into his father's body when he needed one. How it then followed a path to his mother.'

'Followed a path?'

Martyn was talking exactly as if he knew how a Ka behaved. How could this be?

'Yes, that's exactly what it did.'

What it did. He must know a lot about the Ka. He continued, contemptuously.

'After Jim had to say Goodbye Cruel World, Father Grey was on hand. The old guy used to be the parish priest for little Stevie and his mother during the war years, before she flipped. Added to that, Father Grey employed Ken, the son of Jim's close friend Tommy Barker.

'Trouble is, his health was, to say the least, wobbly. Fortunately, the lovely Victor Smith was on hand to lead the way to Mavis. I haven't been able to discover exactly what Smith's link to Mavis was – something dark, no doubt – but there was one.

'And, before you start wondering where Bryony Richards fits in with Steve's history, she doesn't. You just happened to be the only one available when Mavis breathed her last. Thought she'd live forever, that one did. Well, no-one does, not really, except as a Ka. The Ancient Egyptians knew something about that. Even Stephen Charles was right about that much at least.'

How could he, Martyn, know all these things? His study of the Ka must have been exhaustive.

'Now it's time for the next link in the chain to be formed,' Martyn continued. 'A deliberate, properly thought-through one this time. I'm going to take over Stevie boy's Ka. This will be the moment my life has been leading towards for all these years.'

Unbidden, an image leaped into my mind. It was of me, as Jim Corcoran, reading a book in Wandsworth Prison sixty years ago and learning something about the Ancient Egyptian belief.

'Just think of it,' he said. 'It must be the next best thing to living forever. And you've wasted your chance. Well, I won't do the same. I've already thought of a few things to make Martyn Bedford a success like the World has never seen before. And, in twenty, thirty years or whenever it might be, I'll just carry on as someone else.'

'Martyn,' I said. 'It doesn't work like that. There's a cacophony of voices going on within you if you host to a Ka. You don't know who you are half the time. You, as you are now, won't have much control over what happens.'

'You lot might not have been able to do it. But just look at yourselves – a boy going nowhere in life, a man whose life had been wrecked by what happened during the war, a Parish Priest with some sort of saint complex who was already on his way out, a sub-human with an overdeveloped sex drive and not much else, a woman who had degenerated into a tramp.

'Then of course came you, Bryony. I'll leave you to describe yourself. Or maybe I'll be kind and say it's true: you're certainly not the person you were before Mavis died in your arms.

/Once you were a capable person. I even admired you. Now, for some reason, you've become nothing but an ageing bag of hormones. Still, it did make things easier for me.

'With me, things are going to be so different. I know exactly what I'm doing. It'll at last be like the Ka having a new and more competent pilot taking over at the helm – one who is sure about where he's going and knows how to steer the ship. It'll be nothing more than that.'

'Ka...'

This was the only word I could get out. I couldn't say more, nor could I understand or even properly hear much of the rest of what Martyn was saying.

He was still speaking when I could hear no more.

[7] Martyn

Curse the woman.

Bryony Richards was right. This is exactly like living in too close contact with six noisy people. She told me it wasn't like being the helmsman of a ship. Well, it is – one with a quarrelsome, rebellious crew.

This cacophony of voices has even been muddling my thoughts on the money-making schemes I once had.

The bank balance of Bryony Enterprises is diminishing ever further. The company still is my main source of income, although the woman herself has been gone for years. Its value is about half of what it was the day after the kindly Dr Fischer had taken the greater part of its financial assets off my hands.

*

By the time of the fifteenth anniversary of Bryony's departure, the fretful personalities within me became worse than ever. It's hard to say which one of these deranged people is the worst to deal with.

The dreary drone of Hubert Green has lately been at its worst. Last week the priest tricked me into doing some voluntary work. Voluntary work!

Most depressing are the hours when I have to endure the mournful regrets of Jim Corcoran. Is it my fault that his life went so wrong on a beach in northern France all those years ago?

Between them, all six are driving me mad.

It was a vain hope that moving from London to the city where I went to university, way back in the Twentieth Century, would somehow put me more in touch with the future than the past. No such luck. Still, Oxford does at least feel like a young city with all the people on the threshold of life around me.

At first, I felt sure I would be tipped over the edge, but I did somehow manage to find a way of living with the hubbub within me. Gradually, I began to learn to regard myself as a kind of manager-nurse for a bunch of delinquents. After all, they couldn't do much without my co-operation.

A few months ago. I hit on the idea of treating them all, one-by-one, to the luxury of being allowed to write down their stories. I'd like to say this was out of the kindness of my heart, but the truth is that I'd hoped this would quieten them all down.

And it did work, although only for a short time. Every one of them – even the animal that was Victor Smith – waited politely for the others to take their turns. Then, as soon as Bryony had written her last word, they all became worse than before. It really is driving me crazy this time.

Now I've decided to take a turn to set my own, Martyn Bedford's, tale down. I soon decided to confine my writing to these brief notes, limited to the time after Bryony's death. I didn't want to revisit my earlier years. I'm not looking for sympathy. During the time when Mavis and Bryony were, in a sense, the pilots, my life was all about doing the work – believe me, there was a lot of it – to lead to where I am now. Leading up to this state of affairs!

Maybe I was a tiny bit pleased to find how close most of their stories were to what I'd been able to find out. Still, even if I say so myself, I had been painstaking and thorough with my research.

*

A fortnight ago, I made the decision it was now time for Martyn Bedford to make his own exit. He's nearly seventy years old now, after all. Time to hand over to someone younger. Next week, Saturday 26th May 2040 to be precise, will see the first day of the centenary of the Dunkirk evacuation. I've decided he should make way for his successor before then.

He won't be missed by anyone. Martyn Bedford as such, I mean. He'll simply take his more rational place alongside the other six. He'll be able to offer a cooler perspective on the way forward than that confused bunch of people ever could.

At the very least he'll be an ally, not a hindrance, to the new, carefully selected, person who'll take over at the helm. Together, the two might even be able to make them all shut up.

You see, I am now able to think of Martyn Bedford quite neutrally as 'he'. This is because I've already selected my successor. Well, at least I have a shortlist of two young people – students in this old City, they are. I'll be deciding later today which of them will be the lucky one.

Both are highly intelligent people. They're ambitious and have the necessary streak of ruthlessness within them. Both share my vision of the future to a remarkable degree. Either will, I hope, have within them exactly what it takes to see things through.

I never had children myself – too busy with work – but I think of Emma Price and Noah Harley as my surrogate daughter and son. It will be hard to choose between them. It's probably as well they don't know of the prize that awaits one of them.

Whichever it is will be surprised, to say the least, when I commit suicide in front of them. Don't worry; I have all the details carefully worked out.

Emma and Noah aren't their real names, naturally. As I said to begin with, none of the names set down here are the real names. Nor are any of the places those in which the events happened. Except for Dunkirk, of course.

The lucky person I'm going to choose might even be you.

oOo

,

Recently by Tom East

NOVELS
The Gospel According to St Judas
The Greenland Party
The Lowell Letters
Tommy's War: July, 1914

THE ELDRITCH COLLECTIONS
The Eve of St Eligius
Wish Man's Wood

NON-FICTION
A Fifties Childhood
Lightning Strikes Twice
Why Write Haiku?

POETRY
Scenes from Seasons
Charge of The Light Verse Brigade
Lyrics, Polemics & Poetics

Coming next:
The Answer is an Egg Sandwich